House of Virgil

Chance Prosser

I dedicate this book to the memory of my grandfather,
Robert Prosser

CONTENTS

Magic is real.

Don't ask me how it works, or what magic is. I don't know a lot about magic; I just know that it exists. Magic is magic, and that's how it functions. So, to all of you disbelievers, the sooner you accept that something illogical and unexplainable is possible, the sooner you can actually enjoy the story I have for you--the story of not only how I came to discover magic, but also how I learned how to use magic.

My name is Simon Crowley, although a lot of people probably remember me as THE STYLISH SIMON, but I'll get back to that in a moment. First, I wanted to talk a little about my past. I'm well known for my charming exaggeration, but what I am writing now is the complete truth. I don't want anyone doubting my claims, especially with how absurd they may seem (I'm looking at you, disbelievers of magic).

I was born and raised in Santiago's Shield, California. To those of you who have never heard of it before, I don't blame you. Sure, it's a big city, but it's no San Francisco or Los Angeles. But it was my home, so I definitely have a certain attachment to Santiago's Shield. And when you live in the slums of the city like I do, that's saying something.

My family situation was never the greatest. Of course, when you have six other siblings, that's a given. My parents made the choice to get married immediately after they graduated from high school, and four months later, I was born (I try not to look too much into timing and I've never asked about it). I'm not blaming my parents for anything-- they're good people who do go out of their way to provide for their children--but we were barely getting by.

So, after I turned sixteen, I made the wonderful choice to drop out of high school to help provide for the family. Of course, poor decision-making runs in the family.

It was hard to find work being a teenage dropout who lacked skills for the workforce, so I turned to being a street performer. I picked up a knack for stage magic and started earning pocket change as THE STYLISH SIMON!

Then, one day, someone came and ruined the show, by showing me true magic.

Chapter 1

"When he turned around, he subtly marked the green crayon on his right ring finger. While he waved his hands around the young boy's head, he took a glance at his nails." A voice called out from the crowd.

Simon held back a shocked gasp and quickly scanned the crowd. There were around a dozen people watching, and although he was not able to identify who called him out, he recognized the frowns on their faces. What really tore him up was the boy who saw the green mark on his hand and started to tear up. The child's parents took him away, shaking their heads in disapproval.

The mind reader act was a simple trick on Simon's end. He kept his back to the volunteer and asked them to pick a crayon to place in his hands. He turned around afterwards, making it obvious that he was not taking a glance at the crayon. And just as the stranger said, when the volunteer handed him the crayon, he marked his fingernail with it to know its color and returned it. The hand waving over their heads was just to see his fingernail. He was thankful that none of his siblings were around. That was Sabrina's favorite trick and he would hate for it to be ruined for her.

Of course, he still had an audience, so the show must go on.

"The Stylish Simon isn't done yet!" he declared with a confident grin. "And I think that someone in the audience needs to cool down. For my next trick, I shall turn water into ice!"

The audience looked on as Simon turned around to reach into his backpack. He pulled out a coffee mug, a small bowl, and a bottle of water. He was certain that this trick would at least shut up the stranger. It was the end of August, and it was a very hot day on top of that. The act, which he dubbed as "cool as ice," would be enough to win back his audience.

Simon set the bowl down on the sidewalk. Then, he held the coffee mug in one hand, and a bottle of water in the other. With his teeth, he bit around the bottle cap and twisted it off. He started to whistle a playful tune as he began to pour the water into the mug until the bottle was completely empty. To the audience, it was obvious that the mug would overflow before the bottle was half empty, but it never did. If that was not enough to amaze the audience, what came next would be. Simon knelt by the bowl and tilted the mug.

Twelve ice cubes fell from the mug and into the bowl.

"And we have ice!" Simon declared, bowing to the clapping and collected gasps. "Thank you! Thank-"

"There is a sponge at the bottom of the mug," the already-familiar voice of the stranger interrupted, "The ice was always there."

Simon frowned yet another one of his tricks was ruined. This time, he was prepared, and finally identified the stranger. Of course, that was partially because the rest of his audience was now moving on. The stranger was a middle-aged man, wearing a dark red trench coat and brown dress shoes. He had his gray hair slicked back and looked at Simon with piercing yellow eyes. He kept a stoic expression on his face, not exposing his emotions as Simon did, who glared at the older man in anger.

Finally, Simon sighed. The show was over, thanks to this man. He dumped the half-melted ice onto the street drain and placed the bowl and mug back into his backpack, which held the rest of his props. He threw the empty water bottle into a nearby trash can and picked up his top hat. Within it were a few dollars and a lot of change. On a normal day, he would be able to earn more, but after the stranger ruined two of his acts, he did not feel like continuing. And he was hoping to buy snacks for his younger siblings.

"Can I help you?" Simon asked the stranger, who remained where he was while watching Simon.

"Do you know any magic?" The stranger asked.

"Of course I know magic!" Simon shot back, stuffing his earnings into his pocket. "If you want, I can show you a card trick. It's a real classic and-"

"You have separated your card deck into red and black halves. When I take a card, you will note what half it is from and make sure I put it back in the other half, which you will be able to find."

"I didn't even tell you what card trick I was going to do." That was, however, the card trick Simon had in mind though.

"I knew it was what you had planned," the stranger replied. "Do you know any *real* magic?"

"I have news for you, sir," Simon said as he put his top hat back on. "Magic isn't real."

"How funny it is to see someone with so much potential as a disbeliever."

Simon raised an eyebrow in shock. Disbeliever was a term he commonly used for someone in the audience who was not into his show. He would then pull them up as a volunteer and astound them with another trick. Yet, the stranger seemed to have a different tone when he used disbeliever.

Simon turned around and walked away from the stranger.

Truth be told, Simon was expecting for the stranger to call out to him. Yet, no call ever went out. He turned his head over his shoulder, and sure enough, the stranger was looking at him, as if he was expecting something. Simon took three more steps away from him as they made eye contact. Still, the stranger made no move to stop him. Finally, Simon sighed, and turned back around to face the man.

"How did you know what card trick I was going to do?" Simon asked.

"Magic."

"Uh-huh."

"I read your mind."

"Sure you did."

"Your name is Simon Crowley. Your birthday is on September 16th. You are the eldest child of Phillip and Maria Crowley. Your siblings, by order of birth, are Scott, Samantha, Sabrina, Seth, Samuel, and Sara. You perform what you call magic on the streets to make money, specifically for your siblings. I would ask if I have proved that I've read your mind, but you are fairly confident that I am a stalker."

"H-how?!" Simon gasped.

"And now you're starting to believe me," the man continued.

"Get out of my head!" Simon exclaimed.

"My apologies," the stranger bowed his head, eyes closed. "I was simply proving my point."

"Point proven," Simon sighed out in relief. "So, why did you ruin my act?"

"As I said, you have potential."

"Potential? You mean, I have potential for--and I can't believe I'm saying this-- real magic?"

"Of course."

Simon put both of his hands on his head, trying to process what was happening. There was something off about the stranger, yet there was no being able to explain what it was he was doing. There was no way he could read his mind, yet that's exactly what he had done. Hesitantly, Simon took a step back, away from him. He had no clue who he was dealing with, but what he did know was that whoever the man was, he was certainly dangerous.

"No thanks," Simon muttered. "If you were busy reading my mind, you would know that I don't exactly have the time to give up my life to study magic, or whatever it is you're pulling on me."

"It seems you have plenty of time," the stranger countered. "All you really do is perform on the streets and spend time with your family. If you had an actual job or didn't drop out of school, I would take that into consideration."

"Was that a burn?" Simon asked, crossing his arms.

"It is what it is," the stranger replied without emotion, although there were hints of a smirk on his lips. "If you are interested in my offer--"

"I'm not interested."

"--then you will have to leave your life, although not for good. Just for a year, at least-"

"Still not interested."

"--and then perhaps you will have the talent to make money for your siblings."

"That would have gotten my interest, if I had any reason to believe you. You don't seem like someone with a steady income."

"Check your hat."

Simon paused for a moment, then decided to humor the stranger. He grabbed his top hat and pulled it off. He was shocked to see that it was now filled to the brim with stacks of dollars. At first, he questioned how that money even got into his hat without his knowledge, but then, he saw that each bill was worth one hundred dollars. It took a great performance and an over enthusiastic fan to get a five. Now, he had tons of money to share with his family. Simon could not hold the joy as his jaw dropped with a wide smile. The stranger offered a kind smile. It was seeing the stranger that snapped Simon back to his senses.

"Where did you get all of this?" Simon asked cautiously.

"It comes from my line of work."

"Right. That doesn't answer my question. Because, if you stole this money, then I shouldn't take it."

"I acquired it legally, and it is my gift to the Crowley family."

Simon paused for a moment. "This is a bribe, isn't it?"

"It is what it is."

Simon just stood in awe, like many of his unexpecting audiences before today. He could not come up with explanations on how the stranger was able to sneak so much money into his hat, nor how he was able to read his mind. Perhaps there was a chance that magic was real. It was possible that this was his path to getting his siblings to a good life, one better than his.

Still, to leave his family behind for a year, at a minimum, was too much. Even if the payout was as good as this, it was not worth leaving behind the siblings that looked out for him or the parents that cared for him. It took a lot of willpower on his end, but he held his hat out to the stranger.

"Take it back," Simon told him. "I... I can't leave."

"Keep the money. It's my gift to you," the stranger told him. "I understand that you are at a crossroads. What you decide to do next will decide how your life turns out. If you take the path you are on, Mr. Crowley, you can go back to your normal life and pretend that this day never happened. But, if you take me up on my offer, your life will never be the same again, as you will dive into the arcane mysteries. I shall give you two weeks to think about this."

"And how will I get back to you if I change my mind?" Simon asked, out of curiosity.

"My card is in your hat."

Simon took a glance down at his hat, and sure enough, a business card was now sticking out. He was about to make a comment towards the stranger when he noticed the stranger was now gone. Of course he would finish off his act with a disappearance; that's exactly what he would have done if he had the resources to pull it off. Simon took the card, and written in red ink, was a single word, with no form of contact information.

"Archmage."

Yes, I made the choice to take the money from the mysterious sorcerer who needed to learn how to make a business card. Don't be so surprised. I already admitted that poor decision-making runs in the family. But to all of you disbelievers: you must admit that what happened was magical. If not, go ahead and explain how he pulled off those tricks to me.

Now, I bet you're wondering if I ended up accepting Archmage's offer at all. I had two weeks to think about it. Well, unfortunately for you, part of being a magician is about building suspense to the audience. Don't worry. I'll answer that question soon, but there's another important matter to bring up.

My family. My family is both the reason why I should take Archmage's offer and why I shouldn't.

Now, I should talk about my parents again. Yes, they did care about me. I'm their child. That doesn't mean we necessarily get along. I mean, would you be alright if your child decided to drop out of high school and become a street performer? I didn't think so (Me? I totally would). They did try to keep me in school too, but that didn't work out so well.

At this point I should say, "stay in school, kids." I am very confident you will not meet an almighty wizard who gives you free money and an apprenticeship. Don't try to be like me. I am one of the worst role models out there.

Moving on, I want to talk about my wonderful brothers and sisters. The thing I am good at is being the best big brother I can. While my parents pay the bills, I give my siblings whatever I earn out on the streets. And of course, they are my biggest fans.

I even remember all of their favorite tricks:

Samantha's favorite trick is another one of those find the card tricks (there's so many different variations).

Sabrina's favorite trick is the mind reading act, as mentioned before.

Seth's favorite trick is breaking a pencil with an index card (not my personal favorite, but he likes it).

Samuel's favorite trick is pulling a coin out of his ear (he's young, give him time).

Sara is too young to understand what I'm doing.

As for Scott, well, out of all my siblings, I'm worried about Scott the most.

Chapter 2

It was around evening that same day when Simon neared his house, carrying two plastic bags. He decided to buy some groceries for his family, along with a couple of surprises for his siblings. It was later than he was supposed to be, so he was hoping that the groceries would be enough to soothe his mother over. His father would work late today, so he did not have to worry so much about him for now.

The Crowley family lived in a small, one-story house, with a small front lawn and foliage covering the back lawn. There was a small attic and a basement that flooded during heavy storms. It was not a very great place to live--and there was not a whole lot of room for nine people--but it was affordable. One day, his family would have better living conditions. He hoped so, at least.

Simon walked up to the worn-out door with a lion-shaped door knocker on it. He used it to knock on the door twice, followed by a single knock a second later.

"It's Simon!"

"Simon's back!"

"Simon! Simon!"

The door opened, and Simon was only able to take a step in before his siblings swarmed over him. From the nine-year old Samantha and Sabrina to the four-year old Samuel, they greeted him with hugs. Simon worked hard to earn the love and admiration of his siblings, from his magic tricks to his gifts. Why else would he go out of his way, and sacrifice his own wants for theirs? It was his desire to make sure they didn't go down the same path as he did. Once he made sure they were all on their way to success, he would be able to start looking after himself.

Simon smiled at his siblings, stepping in. Thankfully, with the gifts of toys he had for them, that was enough to get them off of him. He told them that he needed to speak with their mother. They ran off with their new toys, leaving Simon by himself for once. He made his way to the kitchen, with a small dining table near the fridge, to put away the groceries. While Simon was doing that, his mother entered the room and crossed her arms. She was tired from an early day of work and looking after the children.

"You missed dinner," Simon's mom told him. "We don't have leftovers."

"I got myself some fast food before going shopping," Simon revealed, turning back. "I bought us dinner for the next few days."

"And just how did you get the money for that and, from the joyful screaming, toys?"

In response, Simon walked over to the table and placed his hat down on it, revealing the money within it. His mom looked in awe and worry at the hat.

"How?"

"Well, I'll start at the beginning…"

Simon recounted the events that took place this afternoon regarding his meeting with Archmage. At first, his mother was quick to disbelieve his claims that the stranger knew real magic. She even thought that he had gotten into some sort of trouble to get his hands on that money. It was the business card that saved Simon. It was unique enough to give his story some needed credibility

"I'm not sure if the story is true, but at the very least, you didn't get into trouble," she sighed in relief. "Still, do you think that it's a good idea to run off with this man?"

"Probably not," Simon shrugged. "I don't want to leave home, but when you think about it, it's not like I have a whole lot to do."

"Simon,"

"I'm not wrong," Simon shook his head. "I'm just another mouth to feed here. At least the others have a chance for the future."

"You do know that's entirely of your own doing, right?"

"That it is, Mom, that it is," Simon chuckled. "Just like how whatever I decide to do here will be my own choice.

Whether I stay here, performing the same old tricks over and over, or make something of my life."

"You're not going to run off with a stranger to do that," she told him. "It's too dangerous."

"It is, but sometimes, to get somewhere, you have to take a few risks," Simon smirked. "Now, don't you worry. I'm probably not going to take him up on his offer. However, I do have two weeks to think it over. If I'm gone around then, you'll have an idea on where I went off to. And I'll come by to visit when--"

Simon was interrupted by a crashing sound coming from outside. He and his mother moved towards the window to see what was happening. There was a trio of teens getting off their bikes after knocking down a trash can. Simon frowned, recognizing them as old acquaintances back from his high school. They were the troublemakers, the ones who didn't care about the rules, even minor laws. Unlike them, he had respect for the law, and never made the mistake of hanging out with them. Unfortunately, someone was making that mistake.

"Scott…" Simon's mom sighed

"Hang on a moment. I'll get him inside."

Simon walked back to the table to dump the money out of his hat and put it back on. Afterwards, he made his way outside. He opened the door, and his eyes were immediately drawn to his younger brother, who was part of the trio. Scott had the same slim build as Simon did, although he was starting to bulk up a little. While the rest of the Crowleys had black hair, Scott had his dark hair bleached blond. He wore a black jacket, torn jeans, and no helmet.

Fourteen-year old Scott had just entered high school. Already, he was going down the wrong track. Simon was aware of the reputation his friends had. He saw some of the fights they got into in the hallways. He was even targeted a couple of times on the streets when he started performing. They would surround him, attack, and take any money he earned.

The leader of the gang happened to be present at the scene. Simon was trying to recall whatever his name was. For some reason, he was thinking Mac. He was a bulky senior with short brown hair who had been held back a year. It was just Simon's luck that Scott happened to befriend him at the start of the school year two weeks ago. He was already a bad influence on his younger brother, but that was going to come to an end tonight.

"Gentlemen!" Simon called out. "You've appeared to have made a mess of my front lawn."

"It was a mess already," Mac snickered.

"That was uncalled for, Mac," Simon frowned.

"My name is Zack," the bulky teen corrected, popping his knuckles. "Zack Attack."

How could Simon forget a name that ridiculous? "My apologies."

"Apology not accepted," Mac grabbed Simon by his shirt and lifted him up from the ground. "You know what I'm about to do to you, magic man?"

"Zack, don't," Scott spoke up.

"Oh? You want to do the honors?" Zack grinned.

"Don't worry, Scottie," Simon smiled. "I have him right where I want him. I can take him."

"You really think so?" Zack asked, snorting.

"He doesn't," Scott stepped forward. "Look, man, he's not worth it. Besides, I'm pretty sure my mom's watching, phone in her hands."

"You're right," Zack dropped Simon down onto the ground. "We'll just get him tomorrow."

"I'll be waiting, and I'll be prepared."

"With what? One of your magic tricks? I'm so scared!"

"You should be! I am the Stylish Simon, and my magic is unmatched!"

"Unmatched in how pathetic you are!"

Zack got onto his bike and rode off with the other member of the gang, both laughing. Simon shook his fist at them as they rode off. In immediate hindsight, it was probably a bad idea to pick a fight with Zack, who had already mugged him on multiple occasions. He was most definitely going to keep an eye out for a gang of high school bikers tomorrow. Simon glanced towards his brother, and noticed that Scott was looking away, his cheeks red in embarrassment. He dragged his bike over to the house to chain it up.

"You really want to hang out with a jerk like him?" Simon asked, frustrated. "I remember him. He's not good for you. He's a bully going nowhere with his life. I mean, you think that the man who has been held back a year is going to be successful in life?"

"I think he'll be more successful than the boy who dropped out."

There was a moment of silence as Simon felt the pain to his chest.

"Low blow, Scottie, that hurts. You know why I had to drop out."

"Please, don't call me Scottie," Scott's cheeks became more flushed. "Especially not in front of the others."

"That's our thing, though," Simon argued back, hands on his hips. "You were my assistant once. You remember that?"

"I do," Scott nodded. "And I grew out of that. Magic isn't real."

"It is real!"

"Yeah right."

"No, I mean, the magic I use is fake. But I saw real magic today! A man read my mind, and then conjured up money and a business card and--"

"Simon," he interrupted, "you don't have to impress me. I'm not a kid anymore, so please, stop trying to look after me."

"Scottie--"

"I said to stop calling me that."

Scott turned his back to Simon and walked up to the door.

"I left you a gift in the kitchen. It's a video game for your--"

"Whatever."

Scott opened the door and closed it shut. Simon sighed and looked down at the ground. Once upon a time, the two were close to each other. Now, it feels like they are more distant than ever before. Scott had served as Simon's assistant, but that position was short-lived when the younger brother discovered magic wasn't real. That created a rift between them, and now Scott was going down a darker path than his older brother. Simon's greatest fear was that his siblings would waste their lives and potential, and that was exactly what Scott was doing with Zack.

Suddenly, Archmage's offer was becoming more tempting. If he could show Scott that magic was real, maybe that would be enough to heal their relationship. If he could learn magic, he would be able to support his siblings and their dreams. He would be able to protect himself from Zack and his goons as well. It was still a tough decision to make. Aside from Scott, his family would hate to see him go, but one day, they might be able to understand. Simon yawned and decided to sleep on it. And with sleep on his mind, he returned to his house for some shut eye.

Now, to answer your next question, yes, I did decide to accept Archmage's offer. I was still rather skeptical of it, but if it could help my family, then it would be worth it in the long run. I thought that making that choice would be the hardest part about my future. I was sorely mistaken.

You see, Archmage left me a business card that didn't have any contact information on it. Just his name. That's all I had to go with. I've tried to use it to find him. I said it out loud. I concentrated on his name really hard. I went back to where we first met. I even said his name in front of a mirror three times to see if that would work.

What kind of recruitment agent gave a deal of a lifetime to someone only to never get back in touch with them?

Archmage had pulled off what was arguably one of the greatest disappearing tricks of all time. He showed up, put on a show, and left without a trace. I was disappointed that was how it went down, but I had to admit that he certainly had style (and I should know a little thing about style as THE STYLISH SIMON!). Too bad that now I was ready to take him up on his offer but would never be able to tell him.

So, my life went back to normal, as if I'd never met Archmage to begin with. Except for the money that he left us. My parents put that towards helping the family out, of course. I knew that there was such a thing as real magic, but without any way to act on it, there was not a whole lot I could do. So, for the most part, I went back to my daily routine.

Of course, I ended up having to change up where I performed. Zack Attack (still a ridiculous nickname) and his gang were looking for me.

Funny enough, in my attempts to avoid Zack, the two weeks went by swiftly. Then, he finally found me.

Chapter 3

"Thank you! Thank you!" Simon bowed, once again on the streets. The audience clapped after his latest trick, with a few throwing pocket change into his hat. "Now, for my next trick--"

"There he is!"

Simon gasped, hearing the voice of Zack from the side.

"Get him!"

"For my next trick, I will vanish before your eyes!"

Simon wished he could pull off a vanishing trick, just like Archmage did at the end of their meeting. Unfortunately, that was not an option. So, instead, he quickly grabbed his hat from the ground and dashed in the opposite direction of where he heard Zack's voice come from. He hated to leave behind his backpack and supplies, free for the taking, but it would just slow him down. His primary goal was to escape at any cost from Zack.

Dashing down the street, Simon took a glance over his shoulder. Zack and four of his friends were after him, riding their bikes. At first, he was surprised that Zack was even out during the early afternoon on a school day. Then again, Simon wasn't surprised that he would have ditched school. At the very least, he was glad that Scott was not with the gang today. There was hope for him. He just needed to get away from Zack to act on that hope.

Simon turned his head back forward to continue to run. He was not going to outrun Zack, not when the gang had bikes. Still, he was smarter than his pursuers. He had a plan. Simon made a left turn, purposely going down a street that went downhill. That was going to give Zack and his gang the momentum they needed to catch up to him. Within a few seconds, they had closed the distance between them. Simon glanced over his shoulder, seeing that Zack was right about to run over him.

Simon threw himself towards the left and fell down, letting the five bikers soar down the hill.

"Damn it!" Zack cursed. "Turn around!"

Simon chuckled lightly after hearing Zack's curse. It was a close call, but it did buy him a few seconds. It was time to finish his escape in style. He picked himself up from the ground and ducked into a nearby alleyway. He thought about running uphill but decided he did not have the energy for it. At the very least, the alleyways would limit their movement on the bikes. They would have to ditch them to catch up with him now.

Simon was familiar with the big streets that he performed on. The alleyways were another story. They were a twisting labyrinth for him. He quickly became lost, with no clue on where he was going or how to turn back. He made a quick turn to the right and came upon a dead end.

"Why is this place so confusing?" Simon thought out loud. "Couldn't they leave signs?"

Simon turned back around, only to find himself face-to-face with Zack and his gang.

"Looks like we have him cornered," Zack grinned.

"Go ahead and take my lunch money," Simon dumped his hat's contents onto the ground and took a step back to put it back on.

"Not what I'm here for, magic man," Zack advanced. "There's no one to call the cops on us now."

"Well, I can," Simon pointed out.

"Since when did you have a phone?" Zack asked before grabbing Simon by his shirt.

"That was a bluff," Simon admitted. "Zack, I'm going to give you one chance to let me go, or I might just have to humiliate you in front of your buddies."

"Go ahead and try."

"If you insist."

Simon was never much of a good fighter. He preferred sweet-talking his way out of trouble, but when push came to shove, he could look out for himself. Simon brought his head forward quickly, slamming his forehead down on Zack's nose. The brute let out a gasp and let go of his victim. Simon did not stop his attack, and swiftly kicked his attacker in the groin. With a scream, Zack fell down on the ground in pain. Simon grinned for a moment, feeling victorious.

Then the four other members of Zack's gang swarmed over Simon and punched the grin from his face.

Simon fell to the ground and assumed an armadillo stance. He placed his hands over the back of his head and curled his legs and head towards his chest. His eyes were closed as he endured the beating from Zack's gang. Fists and feet struck across his body without mercy, seemingly unending. Eventually, they parted ways, only for Zack to start assaulting Simon on the ground. With his nose bloodied and his pride damaged in front of his gang, the brute did not hold back.

"Gentlemen."

The assault came to an end as the gang turned around. Simon picked his head up upon hearing the voice and smiled in relief. Archmage was now present, stepping forward towards the gang and their victim. His yellow eyes analyzed the scene without emotion. The bikers were confused by his presence, wondering just who this stranger was. Simon's smile turned into a grin. He was fully aware of what Archmage was capable of.

"And just who are you?" Zack grunted.

"Not important," Archmage brushed him aside. "I am here to talk with Mr. Crowley."

"You can have him after we're done with him."

"I'm afraid I do not have much time. It should only take a few minutes."

"Tough luck. If you don't feel like waiting, we can stop, but you're in for a world of trouble."

"That won't be necessary. I already know that I do not have time for you."

"Is this guy for real? I think I might just beat you up for the fun of it. How do you like that idea?"

"I highly advise against it."

"Let's get him," Zack declared, cracking his knuckles. His gang started to move forward to surround Archmage.

"Very well. I think I can make time for you."

Simon slowly stood up, leaning on a wall for support. The gang did a number on him with their beating. Archmage allowed them to surround him, showing no hint of fear at their numbers. Instead, he simply unbuttoned his trench coat, wearing a white tunic and brown dress pants underneath it. He tossed his coat back right as Zack charged forward, fist swung outward.

Simon didn't even blink when Zack and his goons went crashing down to the ground.

Archmage, with his trench coat somehow already back on, approached Simon. There was not a scratch on him.

"H-how?" Simon gasped.

"I made time for them," Archmage told him.

"That didn't answer my question!"

"Oh. In that case, I made time by stopping time."

"You stopped time?!"

"I stopped time. For eighteen seconds."

"Eighteen seconds?!"

"I only needed seven to deal with the gang, but I used the rest of the time to put my trench coat back on."

Simon was silent in awe. Archmage's power was amazing to behold in person, he realized. The man motioned to the top hat, which went forgotten on the ground. Simon quickly picked it up as well as collecting the spare change he earned from today's performance. Archmage then held out a familiar backpack to the young teen. By now, he knew better than to question how it happened and took the backpack to sling over his shoulders, across his back.

"Thank you," Simon muttered.

"It is no problem," Archmage replied. "Have you thought about my offer?"

"I have," Simon nodded. "And you really need to put some kind of contact information on your business card."

"I will keep that in mind. What did you decide on?"

"Well, after a lot of thought, I decided to take you up on your offer."

"As expected. And now that you are confident in your answer, I can tell you the cons of training with me."

"Cons?" Simon raised an eyebrow in confusion.

"Yes. To begin with, you will have to leave behind your old life, starting today. You will not be given time to say goodbye to your family. Additionally, there are dark forces at work. There is a war waging beyond the cosmos. You may be asked one day to take part in that everlasting battle, and I will not lie to you when I say it may very well cost you your life."

"Uh-huh. And that's all there is with the cons?"

"Those are the two big ones. There is a third one that applies directly to you, but if I tell you, I know for sure you will turn away and leave now."

"So, I have to accept it now, and find out the third con later?"

Archmage nodded silently. Simon could not even begin to imagine what could be worse than the first two cons. To start off, Archmage flat out told him that he may die if he goes down this path. What could he possibly mean by dark forces waging war behind the scenes? Still, Simon reasoned it could not be that much of a challenge. If he could access even a portion of Archmage's power and talent, that would be enough to make him a mighty warrior. If the veteran sorcerer was able to bring down five brutes with a snap of his fingers, then he could certainly hold his own against whatever the dark forces were.

What did trouble Simon was the fact that he had to leave behind his family. They would question where he went, and they would miss him when they realized he was not coming back. At least, not immediately. Even if Archmage was so confident that he would never see his family again, Simon intended to prove him wrong. If it came down to it, he would leave behind his training, hopefully taking a few tricks with him when he did so. He still had no idea on what the third negative Archmage had in mind was, but soon enough, he would find out.

"I accept," Simon declared.

"Excellent. Please, take my hand."

Archmage extended his hand forward for a handshake

Without hesitation, Simon gripped Archmage's hand firmly.

Their surroundings changed before them in the blink of an eye. They were no longer in the streets, surrounded by unconscious thugs. Now, the two found themselves in a hallway. Steel lockers lined the walls and there were wooden doors that led to individual rooms. Simon released his hand from Archmage's, the realization quickly hitting him.

"This is it?" Simon asked. "This is the third con?"

"It is," Archmage answered. "You're back in school now."

"You gotta be kidding me," Simon facepalmed.

"Now, you will find that the North American Academy for Magicians is unlike any other educational institution,"

Archmage started to walk down the hallway. "For example, we're in a different dimension. A pocket dimension, but still another dimension."

"If we're in a pocket dimension, then why are we named after North America, when we're not actually in North America?"

"Very funny, Mr. Crowley. My office. Now."

Simon could not tell if Archmage was joking or not. He let out a sigh of disappointment. Suddenly, learning magic had become less cool. Archmage being a principal even took away some of his awesome credibility. Regardless, Simon followed suit. It was time to see what this school had to offer him.

I was disappointed when I found out that Archmage was going to put me back in school. I expected that there would be one on one lessons or maybe some magical ritual that unlocks my true power. Nope. It was an actual school, with classrooms and lockers and everything.

I'm all for there being academies for magic, but when you're going to learn about supernatural forces and such, it shouldn't be done in your typical high school. Why not have it in a ruined castle or an antique temple? I mean, the pocket dimension part is cool, but that's all that really makes the North American Academy for Magicians magical.

Now, if we're being real here, I hate school. For the most part, it's just sitting in a classroom for most of the day and learning about something that's likely never going to help you. I don't think all schools are bad. It's good to teach children how to read and write and perform simple math. It's the upper level education that I have a problem with, like middle and high school. They need to do a better job of having students think about what they want to do with their future instead of teaching us that the mitochondria is the powerhouse of the cell and where to put commas. Maybe then I wouldn't think dropping out to perform magic on the streets was a good idea.

Not that it mattered too much. If you took a look at my grades, you would know that I was a pretty terrible student to begin with. And that was because I reached a point where I stopped caring and didn't put any more effort into my assignments. In a way, I'm more street smart than I am book smart. Someone with book smarts would know better than to pick a fight with someone like Zack. Someone with street smarts would find a way to avoid that confrontation to begin with (don't look too much into that fight happening--I tried to avoid it).

Even though I'm not a big fan of school, I wasn't going to throw away this opportunity. If you have to pull one lesson from this (aside from magic being real), it's this: don't throw away a second chance. It gives you the opportunity to make up for the mistakes you've made in the past. Throwing away a second chance is just as bad of a choice as breaking off your first chance. So, I was going to stick through this. Not everyone gets a second chance to make their life better.

Chapter 4

Archmage wasn't kidding when he said he had an office. Simon sat across from the headmaster in a brown leather chair. Archmage sat across from him and filled out some paperwork. There was a desk between them with stacks of paper and an intercom microphone on it. Behind Archmage was a bookcase with thick tomes with a strange language written on the spines. Pictures hung on the back wall as well, each one portraying Archmage with others wearing a similar coat he wore now. Simon assumed that they were colleagues, although he was too distracted to ask.

Simon glanced at the side wall and was surprised to see a window. Outside the window, he was even more amazed to see that the sky was covered in thick purple clouds. It was definitely a sight from out of the world. If Simon had to guess, the purple clouds were likely a result of the school being in a pocket dimension. He was starting to realize that being in a pocket dimension made up for the fact that he was back in school. Pocket dimensions were cool.

Archmage pressed the button on the intercom microphone. "Solomon Brenton. Please have a student who knows their way around the academy report to my office."

"I'm sorry, but is that an actual intercom?" Simon asked.

"A magical one."

"A magical one?"

"That is what I said."

"You're joking." Simon rolled his eyes.

"I am quite serious."

"Oh yeah? Is that pen in your hand a magic pen?"

"Don't be ridiculous, Mr. Crowley. How could a pen possibly be magical?"

Simon couldn't tell if Archmage was being serious or not. He knew a couple of magic tricks that involved a pen, and that wasn't even real magic.

"So, there are students here right now?" Simon questioned. "Does that mean school's in session?"

"Students are moving in as we speak," Archmage answered. "Classes begin tomorrow. There will be a couple of items that you need to take care of beforehand, but for the most part, I can handle that."

"Like what?"

"Your uniform, for example."

"Please tell me the uniforms aren't too formal," Simon sighed out.

"The uniform consists of a trench coat, a white dress shirt, dress pants, and dress shoes. The coat, pants, and shoes will have the same color, which is dependent on what school of magic you decide to pursue first."

"School of magic? But aren't we in a school of magic?"

"Very funny, Mr. Crowley. There are seven fields of magic you can specialize in. There is a pamphlet you can read on the seven schools of magic in your hat."

Simon took a deep breath in, steeling his nerves. He took his hat off his head, and sure enough, there was a pamphlet inside of it. Simon sighed when he noticed Archmage smirking. One of these days, he was going to find out how the principal could accomplish such feats (magic was not an acceptable answer in that regard). He took the pamphlet and started to scan through it.

The North American Academy for Magicians is one of seven magical institutions on Earth to teach magic to the next generation. Like the other six academies, we offer seven fields of study: alteration, combative, displacement, enchantment, foresight, illusions, and support,

Alteration is the study of transformative magic. Magicians who study in alteration are capable of twisting someone so that they are non-threatening or bolster the strengths of their allies. Regina Basil serves as the professor of alteration and the uniform color is blue.

Combative is the study of offensive magic. Magicians who study in combative magic are capable of manipulating magic to serve as a weapon, one which can be precise as well as devastating. Solomon Brenton serves as the professor of combative and the uniform color is orange.

Displacement is the study of transportation magic. Magicians who study in displacement are capable of teleporting themselves and others to a select location as well as summon objects or creatures. Flynn Hawkins serves as the professor of displacement and the uniform color is gray.

Enchantment is the study of domination magic. Magicians who study in enchantment can change the perception of someone to see others as friends or foes as well as control others. Jeremy King serves as the professor of enchantment and the uniform color is yellow.

Foresight is the study of informational magic. Magicians who study in foresight magic can unearth the secrets of the past as well as catch glimpses of the future. Aurora Winter serves as the professor of foresight and the uniform color is green.

Illusion is the study of deceptive magic. Magicians who study in illusion are able to create fake images and sounds as well as project these illusions on the minds of others. Cassandra Murdoch serves as the professor of illusion and the uniform color is purple.

Support is the study of defensive magic. Magicians who study in support magic are capable of projecting magical barriers to protect themselves as well as banish their opposition. Sierra Montague serves as the professor of support and the uniform color is brown.

Simon had been hoping that the pamphlet would reveal more about Archmage's power, but alas, his red coat did not match up to that of the school uniforms. Even the basic descriptions of the fields of magic did not give him an idea. It did leave him with thinking about what field he should pursue. Each one seemed to have its ups and downs, making it a tough decision.

There was a knock on the office door, and with a flick of his wrist, Archmage opened it from his seat. A dark-skinned boy around Simon's age, a few inches taller, entered. He had black hair, gentle green eyes, and broad shoulders. His orange coat marked him as a student of combative magic. He stepped inside, and with Archmage motioning to him Simon stood up.

"Mr. Simon Crowley, meet Mr. Phoenix Brenton," Archmage introduced. "He will serve as your guide for the next day or so."

"Pleased to meet you," Phoenix extended his hand forward.

"Right back at you," Simon took his hand and shook it. "So, Brenton? Any relation to Solomon Brenton?"

"He's my uncle," Phoenix answered with a nod. "It goes without mention that he was my sponsor here as well."

"Sponsor?" Simon raised an eyebrow in confusion.

"A member of the staff must sponsor a potential student for them to enroll here," Archmage told him. "Mr. Brenton, if you would, please lead Mr. Crowley to the boy's dorms."

"Of course, Archmage. Please, follow me."

Phoenix stepped out of the office, and with a nod from the Archmage, Simon followed him. For now, the two walked in silence throughout the hallway. There were other students, ranging from teenagers to young adults. Seeing adults as students was a surprise to Simon, but they wore the same uniforms. However, he also noticed that there were colored badges on their coats. That certainly raised questions.

"So, what's the deal with the older students?" Simon asked. "What's with their badges?"

"Those badges are a sign of proof that they have completed in another field of magic," Phoenix answered. "You see, a student can only study in one field of magic per year. They are only required to have mastered one school of magic, but there are many who want to master them all. Such dedication takes years of study."

"And why would someone want to study magic for that long?"

"It is challenging, but it gives the magician a new status. For example, there is only one man that I know of who has mastered all schools of magic, and he serves as your sponsor."

"We're talking about Archmage, right?"

"Indeed. Speaking of, how did you come to earn his sponsorship?"

"Honestly, I have no clue. He said I had potential, and that was it."

"That may be a question you have to find the answers to on your own."

Simon remained silent, wondering just why Archmage picked him. Just what kind of impression did he make to earn that sponsorship? That question was going to bug him in the back of his mind for days to come.

Phoenix led Simon up a set of stairs. They were in another hallway, although the lockers were now gone. There were only doors, some ajar with conversation and others closed shut. Phoenix led the way about halfway through the hall, then turned to the door to the right. He paused for a moment, then nodded, as if obeying a command from his instructor.

"Is something wrong?" Simon stepped forward.

"Nothing at all," Phoenix brushed aside his concerns with a smile. "This is your room."

"My room? Anything I should know."

"Well, my room is right across from yours. And you have a roommate."

"Of course I have a roommate," Simon groaned out with Phoenix knocking on the door. "So much for not having to share living space with someone else for once."

There was a long pause, then finally, the door unlocked and opened. Standing in the room was a slim and short boy with shaggy blonde hair and blue eyes. His green trench coat was unbuttoned and loose around his body. He rubbed his eyes, and upon closer inspection, Simon noted that there were gray bags underneath his eyes.

"Simon Crowley, meet Alvin Oberon," Phoenix stepped aside. "You'll be roommates."

"Alright," Alvin yawned. "I'm going back to my nap."

Alvin stepped back inside, and Simon followed suit. The door closed behind them, leaving Phoenix behind. It was a small room divided down the center. On each side was a single bed, a chest, a nightstand, and a wardrobe. There was a window that looked out to the clouded sky for that wonderful scenic view in the middle, next to another door. Alvin didn't bother trying to get to know his new roommate at all. Instead, he fell back onto his bed, and within seconds, started to snore. Simon shook his head for a moment, then walked over to his side of the room.

"It's going to need a little bit of work," Simon noted, tossing his backpack down. "But I can manage."

Simon Crowley. Have you thought of what field of magic you wish to pursue?

"What?! Archmage?! Is that you?"

It is.

"Of course. You're using some magic spell to contact me, aren't you?"

Actually, I am using the intercom. As long as I keep a hold on the button, I can speak into the mind of the first person's name I say out loud.

"And of course the intercom is magical."

That's what I told you.

"Yes, I remember."

And do you remember my question? What field of magic would you like to pursue?

"Well, I had some time to think about it, and I have made my decision. I want to study illusions."

Very well. I will finish preparations for your course of study.

"Let me guess. I'm going to open my wardrobe, and there are going to be purple uniforms inside."

And textbooks in the chest.

Simon sighed, then smiled. Archmage was definitely an eccentric magician, but in the end, he was thankful for him.

Why illusions?

To start off, purple's my favorite color.

I'm completely serious. That was something that I considered. If my uniform's color was going to be dependent on what school of magic I pursued, I wanted it to be something I liked as well as something I could pull off. And for the record, yes, I look amazing in purple.

People tend to associate it with royalty and ambition. A lot of people might think it's a stuck-up color. I never thought of it like that. Instead, I saw it as one of the more magical colors. That's what initially drew me to like purple.

Plus, purple has other meanings too. Like, if you break down purple, what do you have? Red and blue. Red is a fierce and aggressive color. Blue is a calm and soothing color. Combine them together, and you get purple. So, purple can be both calm and peaceful, as well as aggressive when it needs to be. In a way, that's like me.

Now, enough about colors and their meanings. I would be an idiot if I picked illusions solely based on the uniform color (I mean, I'm not bright, but I at least know better than that). So, while it was the color that initially had stood out to me, it was the potential it had that held my interest

I'm a street performer, but after a couple of months, I started having bigger dreams. I dreamt of standing in front of larger audiences, on a stage, and astounding them with my magical tricks. Unfortunately, while I, as THE STYLISH SIMON, had a charm for that, I was far behind on the talent portion.

Enter the school of illusion.

If I could master illusions, that opened up a new world of opportunity for me. I would be able to set myself apart from the competition because all of my magic tricks would be actual magic. When I summoned up an illusion, people would wonder how, and I would say "a magician never reveals his secrets." That's what I envisioned for myself from my choice. I had a long-term plan in mind for my education.

Now, there may be others who have this same idea. Maybe some of the other magicians were actually using actual magic to secure their fame. If that was the case, how would I be able to compete against them?

It was my charm that would put me above them. Now, I know you're getting tired of reading this, but I am THE STYLISH SIMON! And that was going to my shot to fame.

Chapter 5

By now, Simon knew better than to question how Archmage managed to get his measurements for the school uniform. It was a good fit for him, and he looked good in it, and that's all that he really needed to think about. He briefly tugged at the edges of the purple coat, wondering who came up with the idea to have trench coats as the school uniform. The coat itself was a deep purple, which was just what Simon was looking for.

Within the hour, Simon would attend his first class to study how to create illusions. He skimmed through the textbooks Archmage had given him to get an idea on what he was going to study (despite being a pocket dimension, the academy still followed Earth's time). Many were the personal journals of illusionists of the past, recounting the illusions they have created over the years.

Additionally, a thick tome recounted the theories of illusion, as well as magic in general. Apparently, anyone could learn magic with enough training. That would be something he would keep in mind for the future. The one book he did not find was one that told him how to cast illusions.

"The house of Virgil the Damned is in jeopardy."

Simon jumped and turned to face Alvin, who had

suddenly spoken. His roommate, who had been asleep, now had his eyes wide open. Simon was not sure what was up with his new roommate. Alvin spent most of yesterday sleeping. Simon thought he would sleep through the night as well, but he was awake and sitting on his bed. And then, for most of the morning, he was asleep. Simon returned from breakfast to get fully dressed when Alvin gave that cryptic warning.

"Virgil the Damned?" Simon asked.

"Virgil the Damned?" Alvin repeated, in a questioning tone.

"That's what you said."

"I don't remember that," Alvin shrugged and sat up on his bed. "Did I miss breakfast?"

"Err, you did," Simon scratched the back of his head in confusion. "I didn't think I should wake you up."

"You're a great roommate, you know." Alvin said flatly.

"I honestly cannot tell if you're sincere or sarcastic. I hope sincere."

"I don't know either. Let's go with sincere."

Simon opened his mouth to respond to that, but after a moment of thought, let out a sigh. All of these magicians were confusing to him. First Archmage, and now Alvin. At least Phoenix was normal enough, compared to the rest of the magicians at the academy.

After getting adjusted to his new room yesterday, Simon had Phoenix show him around the rest of the academy. He made a mental note to remember the illusion classroom. The only other places that came to mind were the dining hall (which he had visited this morning and was disappointed to see it was just a typical school cafeteria) and the library. According to Phoenix, there wasn't really anywhere to go to hang out, but many students study in the library or eat in the dining hall together.

Alvin put on his coat and the two students left their room together to head to class. Eventually, they parted paths. Alvin was a student in the school of foresight and had different classes than Simon. He was not sure what to expect from his class in terms of students. Still, he was rather confident in his ability to fit in. Archmage picked him, so he had that much going for him.

The illusions classroom had three sections. The teacher had her own section in a small corner, fit with a wooden desk, chair, and podium to speak at. There were lines and rows of desks taking up a good portion of the room. Finally, there was a clear space on the other half of the room to practice spells, although Phoenix told Simon that casting spells in class would come later in the year.

Students were coming into the classroom, so Simon was quick to take a seat towards the center of the desks. He noted that there were students of all kinds. Teenagers were the youngest with a few young adults with badges on their coats joining in as well. There were both men and women among the students, along with different origins for each one. Simon doubted that he would get the chance to get to know anyone in the class well. That's how it went for him back at high school, and he expected it to be the same here.

Eventually, the esteemed illusion professor arrived. She was, at most, four feet tall with heavily wrinkled skin and balding silver hair. She wore a dark purple trench coat that dragged onto the ground and walked with a crooked black cane. Her eyes were closed shut as she walked up to be in front of the podium. The students, Simon included, were surprised by how their teacher looked.

"Good day, class. I am Professor Murdoch," she spoke with a high-pitched and nasally voice. "Before we begin class, we have a student violating the dress code already."

Simon tried to spot which student Professor Murdoch referred to. Then, he realized that the rest of the class was looking at him, or specifically, his top hat.

"Of course there's a no hat rule," Simon sighed out. "Professor, I wasn't given any explanation of the rules."

"Well, it's a classroom rule specifically," Professor Murdoch answered, pointing her cane at the hat. "Take it off."

"I did not know it was going to be a big deal."

"Well, it's certainly a big deal now, because your ridiculous hat is on fire."

Simon was about to shoot a comeback at Professor Murdoch when he heard a chorus of gasps from the remaining students. Then, he felt a surge of heat on top of his head. Simon squealed out at the realization and quickly threw his hat off from the brim. Just like Professor Murdoch told him, it was on fire with green flames. In a panic, he quickly started to stomp on the hat, trying to put the flames out, to no avail.

Then, Professor Murdoch snapped her fingers, and the flames went out. There was not even a single burn mark on the top hat, although it was rather beaten up from his foot. The students started to laugh at the display of magic, then broke out into hushed whispers. Simon picked up his top hat, his cheeks burning red from embarrassment. He had forgotten that Professor Murdoch specialized in illusions, and he was never in danger. What a wonderful start to his first day of school.

"Ha, very funny!" Simon joined in on the laugh, trying to brush away his embarrassment. "You got me with that."

"Hat off," Professor Murdoch ordered sternly. "Set it down on my desk. You may collect it after class."

Simon sighed, defeated and humiliated. All eyes were on him as he took the walk of shame to Professor Murdoch's desk. He questioned why she didn't take it herself, as he saw many teachers do with student's phones at his old school. Perhaps she was one for letting students do her work for her. Simon placed his hat on her desk and returned to his seat.

Already, Simon's thoughts turned to payback. He hated it when someone abused their power to humiliate others. At least when Archmage pulled off tricks like this, it was simply to help rather than humiliate. Professor Murdoch fell into the same category as Zack of all people. How he was going to get back at a master of magic with decades of experience was beyond him.

"As you can see, illusions are not just limited to sight," Professor Murdoch lectured. "They change how someone perceives the world. If I were to cast an illusion of a flame on someone's wrist, they would feel the burning on their skin. And with enough training, you will learn to do the same"

"Illusions are capable of so much. You can turn someone invisible or hide your true self. You can mimic sights, sounds, and smells. Illusions are meant to distract rather than to harm. To deceive whoever comes in your way. With enough training, you can look into someone's mind for a brief moment, to bring their greatest dreams to life… or their greatest fears."

Professor Murdoch snickered devilishly with her last statement.

"Now, for the most part, illusions do have one weakness. It is a general rule that if you touch the illusion, you see it for what it truly is: a deception. There are some exceptions to that rule, as with all magic, but those exceptions are for more experienced magicians. If that does not suit your wants, then I highly suggest moving to take displacement instead."

And so, Professor Murdoch droned on with her lecture, going on with many other theories. Because of her voice, Simon found it hard to concentrate. He was likewise distracted with his thoughts. However, he slowly came upon a realization. His lips curled up into a smirk. If his hunch was correct, it was going to make for one great show.

When class came to an end, the students all left the classroom. Professor Murdoch remained in front of the podium, her head following Simon when he walked to her desk. He grabbed his hat and tended to it. He hated how he damaged it, but his teacher was to blame. And now, he was about to make a great discovery or a great mistake.

"Professor Murdoch?" Simon looked over his shoulder.

"Yes?" She turned her body to face him.

"Think fast!"

Simon threw his hat at Professor Murdoch like a frisbee. It sailed through her and the image of the old woman started to flicker.

A slow clap came from the back of the room. Simon turned towards an empty desk, and slowly, a tall woman appeared, wearing the same trench coat as her illusion She was much younger than the image of Professor Murdoch, around her thirties or forties. She had short black hair in a ponytail and a strange red marking over her right eye. She stood up from the desk and grinned at the student.

"Well done, Simon," the real Professor Murdoch finished her clap. "How did you know?"

"You left subtle hints," Simon started while picking up his hat. "You were careful not to touch myself or my hat, and you said illusions cannot touch physical objects. Likewise, even though I'm new to the magical world, I thought that your illusion facade was a little far out there. Finally, Professor Murdoch is a master of illusions."

"That I am, and please, call me Cassandra. Professor makes me sound old. I see now why Archmage sponsored you. I wanted to test his decision and I was wrong."

"So, will you stick with the illusionary teacher trick?" Simon asked, brushing off some dirt from his hat.

"Of course I will. Aside from personal reasons, there's a lesson in it. An illusionist should use their illusions to cause an enemy to underestimate them and to waste their resources. Count that as your first real lesson on the application of illusion."

"And what if a student thinks about revealing your deception?" Simon smirked.

"It wouldn't be the worst to happen," Cassandra shrugged, then chuckled. "But, in exchange for you keeping a secret, I'll grant you a minor favor."

"All I need is one favor," Simon told her, and slowly placed his hat on his head. "The hat stays."

The weeks passed by, and thankfully, Professor Murdoch, or Cassandra, as she wanted to be called when no other students were around, allowed me to wear my hat in class. Even though I would never be able to return the feeling of humiliation by exposing her, it was a small victory.

Now, you may be wondering what's so special about my hat.

Nothing is special about the hat. I just like the look of it.

That's right. There's nothing to it. It's not a gift from a sister, an inheritance from my grandfather, or a sign of affection from a memorable fan. I found my top hat while window shopping, thought I would look good in it, and bought it. That's all there is to my hat.

Back when I was in high school, in English, we talked about what the author meant with their writing. For example, we talked about the meaning of why they made the character's room blue. I mean, come on. Can't a man have a blue room without being psychoanalyzed? Small details don't have to be important to the story at all.

I mean, I couldn't be THE STYLISH SIMON without the hat, but that's all there is to it.

What does the unimportance of my hat have to do about what's coming next? Because the next part is going to recount my seventeenth birthday!

What's so special about turning seventeen? Normally, absolutely nothing (I have a feeling this is going to be quoted whenever someone turns seventeen).

Don't judge me. I'm the one telling the story, and I'll tell it however I like to. But, to satisfy the book critics (and the disbelievers), allow me to tell you that something does happen that pushes the story a little further on its tracks.

Where is it? Read to find out.

What it is? Read to find out.

And just like that, I have my readers hooked on reading about my birthday. That wasn't hard at all

Chapter 6

The day had been too quiet for Simon's liking. It was well into the afternoon (he was judging time based on when meals were served) and there was nothing special happening. Cassandra (still using the Professor Murdoch illusion) was teaching the class how to create simple illusions, such as small animals. There was a lot of studying on how these animals act to make the illusion more realistic. Simon looked forward to incorporating such tricks into his routine, but his thoughts were drawn to how boring his birthday was so far.

Right now, Simon was resting on his bed, bored out of his mind. Alvin was likewise in his own bed, although he was actually trying to sleep. By now, Simon thought that they were friends. Sure, Alvin spent most of the time sleeping, but the few conversations they had were civil. Short, but civil. Perhaps Alvin would be able to help cure his boredom.

"You awake, Alvin?" Simon sat up on his bed.

"I am. Trying to change that."

"Mind if we talk?" Simon offered. "I really need something to do, and there's not a whole lot to do."

"Whatever."

"So, you know, today's my birthday. I'm seventeen today."

"Happy birthday." Alvin spoke in a flat tone.

"Thank you. Now, as I was saying, there's not a whole lot to do. I want to make this day special."

"Well, why not make it special?"

"You have a point. I have to make it special myself! And there's only one way to do that!" Simon shot up from his bed. "Come on!"

"Do I have to?" Alvin groaned.

"You don't want to miss out on this," Simon grinned.

"Well, not like I can get to sleep right now anyways."

Alvin was slow and lethargic, but eventually, he got up. The two teenagers put on their coats. Simon made sure to grab his backpack full of his (fake) magic supplies. He had yet to have a chance to truly show off his tricks ever since arriving at the North American Academy. Even though he was learning real magic, it never hurt to go back to the basics. Especially since everyone here already knew how real magic works, but his tricks would be new.

And the perfect man to test them out on was right across the room.

The two left their room, and immediately, Simon knocked on Phoenix's door. After waiting several seconds, there was no response. If he had to guess, his good friend was likely trying to study in the library. It was time to interrupt that study break. Simon led the way towards the library, followed by Alvin.

The two arrived at the library together. There were long tables from one end of the room to the other with students reading and having light conversation. There were tall bookcases in rows throughout the room. They contained the stories of ancient magicians as well as fictional depictions of magic as the "disbelievers" (the term used to describe people who don't believe in real magic) see it.

In the back of the room was an ominous black door that was locked. Phoenix once told him that was where they kept outdated textbooks, but Simon knew better than that. The door was definitely hiding some kind of secret. Even though he was curious, he had no reason to break the rules to find out what was behind the door.

"There he is," Simon waved towards Phoenix, who was by himself at the end of the table. "Phoenix!"

"Simon, Alvin," Phoenix greeted the two when they sat down at his section of the table. "Can I help you two?"

"As part of my birthday today, I am about to put on a show to amaze the two of you, the friends I've made here so far!" Simon proclaimed.

"We're your only friends here?" Phoenix questioned, concerned. "What about the students in your class?"

"They won't talk to me after the professor humiliated me," Simon shrugged. "So I have you two, and that's all I need. Phoenix, I think I have my answer for why Archmage picked me."

"And what's that?"

"That I already knew about the world of magic before I was taken in!"

To emphasize his point, Simon reached into his backpack and pulled out a ring that hung on the middle of a string. He held it out for both Phoenix and Alvin to see and started to pull on both ends of the string. The ring seemingly defied gravity and started to rise up rather than descend. He had been expecting gazes of awe from his two friends but only received blank looks.

"You dragged me out of bed for this," Alvin sighed. "You're not even using an illusion for this."

"It's amazing, I know," Simon continued to grin. "Just like the Archmage, I can manipulate the laws of the world to-_"

"You're using a rubber band," Phoenix pointed out.

Slowly, Simon lowered the ring and rubber string. "Really?"

"It's obviously plastic," Phoenix told him. "You really should stick to what you learn."

"I liked it!"

The group turned their heads to the side. Three seats down from where they were was another onlooker, a teenage girl. Her hair matched the color of her yellow trench coat and she had gentle green eyes. She clapped when they finally noticed her and moved to sit next to Phoenix and across from Simon.

"It wasn't really magic, Morgan," Phoenix sighed.

"But it does take a smart and clever mind to figure out a trick like that," the girl, Morgan, replied back, before shooting a wink at Simon. "Oh, and happy birthday! If you haven't figured it out yet, I'm Morgan Devlin."

"And I am Simon. You're with the school of enchantment, aren't you?"

"Sure am."

"Of course, someone as enchanting as you would be."

Alvin groaned, then quickly covered his head with his arms on the table. "Wake me up when they're done, Phoenix."

"And you're quite the charmer," Morgan twirled a strand of her hair with two fingers. "You should take enchantment next year."

"Maybe I will. Or maybe I'll choose the next one you decide to take."

Simon Crowley. Please report to my office.

Leave it to Archmage to interrupt a special moment like this. Simon sighed, and slowly stood up from his chair.

"Leaving already?" Morgan teased.

"Archmage's calling," Simon told her. "As his prodigal student, I need to answer the call. But this won't be our last time meeting."

"I'll hold you to that."

"Please, get going," Phoenix rolled his eyes, having remained silent throughout the entire exchange.

Simon quickly grabbed his backpack and headed out of the library. He could only wonder at what important reason Archmage had to summon him. It was hard to tell with him sometimes. Although, it had been quite some time since their last talk, at the start of the school year. Simon arrived at Archmage's office and knocked on the door. It opened for him, with the veteran magician seated at his desk.

"Have a seat, Mr. Crowley," Archmage gestured towards a chair.

Simon took a seat across from Archmage. "So, what do you have for me today?"

"To start off, I want to wish you a happy birthday. I managed to get you a gift that's--"

"It's in my hat, isn't it?"

Archmage remained silent, although the smirk on his face was enough of an answer for Simon. He took off his top hat, and just as expected, there was a colorful card inside, the kind that someone could buy for an easy price at a store. He opened the card to see seven signatures and smiled warmly. He had no idea how Archmage managed it, but they were the signatures of his siblings and parents. His father even signed for Sara, the youngest.

Simon frowned when he noticed that Scott's signature was missing. He closed the card slowly and pocketed it.

"When can I go back?" Simon asked immediately.

"Perhaps in May," Archmage told him bluntly. "That's not why I called you here. I wanted to talk about your performance so far."

"Oh, I know this conversation all too well," Simon reclined back in his chair. "Go on and tell me I need to put more effort into my work."

"Actually, you're doing quite well with your education."

"Huh. That's the first I've ever heard that from anyone."

"Cassandra was impressed with you on the first day," Archmage continued. "I heard that you two are on a first name basis now. She doesn't give her name out like that blindly."

"Well, I do know how to impress my audience," Simon grinned.

"And how about friends?"

"I've made two so far. A third one today, actually, before you interrupted me."

"My apologies. And what of your roommate?"

"Alvin? We get along well enough. He has his quirks, as do I. Although, I don't talk in my sleep like he does. I wonder why he keeps dreaming about this Virgil the Damned guy. That's actually worri--"

"Virgil the Damned?!" Archmage interrupted, and Simon was scared to hear the fear in his voice.

"Err, yes. Is something wrong?"

"What exactly did he say?"

"I'm trying to remember, but it was a little while ago and--"

"WHAT DID HE SAY?!" Archmage bursted out.

"The house of Virgil the Damned is in jeopardy!" Simon yelled back. "That's what he said."

The two were silent for what felt like an eternity to Simon. His heart was beating rapidly out of fear. Fear of both the furious Archmage, and whatever it was that had such a powerful magician so scared. The two controlled their breathing, calming down slowly.

"Once more, you have my apologies, Mr. Crowley," Archmage breathed out. "I ask that you keep this matter between us two."

"Sure," Simon hesitantly nodded. "Should I be worried?"

"No, you shouldn't. The matter is well handled."

"Are you sure?"

"You're dismissed, Mr. Crowley. Have a good day."

"You do know you didn't answer my question, right?" Simon pointed out.

"It is what it is."

That did very little to help Simon out. There was something coming, and he wasn't sure if Archmage had it under control. No. He was confident Archmage did not have whatever threat was taken care of. If someone as powerful as him was scared, everyone should be scared. Unfortunately, Archmage would not say anything else, leaving Simon no more to go off of.

Without another word, Simon stood up and walked out of Archmage's office. As he closed the door, he looked over his shoulder to see that the veteran magician had disappeared. After closing the door, he sighed. There was something big happening, and he was going to get to the bottom of it, no matter what.

"The worst they can do is kick me out of this school," Simon muttered under his breath. "And I have the basics of what I need to succeed back home already."

And as promised, the plot moves forward. You're welcome.

Now, I didn't know the trouble I was getting myself into back then. Frankly, I was scared out of my mind and desperate for answers. I wanted to know what was going on and didn't even realize how much I was in over my head.

I only had three clues to go off in my search.

Archmage was terrified.

Alvin was dreaming about what's coming up.

Virgil the Damned is a pretty ominous name.

The first two leads were busts. I couldn't get a chance to talk to Archmage unless he wanted to talk to me. He didn't want to talk to me. As for Alvin, I tried watching him while he slept (creepy, I know, but I was scared). He didn't mention that cryptic line again and whenever I asked him about Virgil the Damned, he kept pointing out that he only knows him because I brought it up to him.

That only left me with Virgil's name, and that was a terrible lead. I mean, why couldn't Alvin or Archmage mention his last name. At least then I could have used Google (not that the North American Academy for Magicians has computers, but you get my point). But no, all I have to work on is "the Damned" and that's so damn vague!

Yes, that was a pun, but I was still frustrated.

Now, I figured I would get into trouble with Archmage if I go around asking random students and professors, it might start raising some sort of alarm. And then, I would be called to the principal's office for some sort of punishment. I liked the good record I had going for me so far, so that wasn't an option.

So, you know what I did? I studied. With all the free time I had, I went to the library. I was looking through all of the books for three straight days. And I couldn't find any mention of Virgil the Damned!

I did notice something peculiar though. There were various accounts of ancient magicians. It reported on their incredible feats and powers, and they were all of good nature. But where were the magicians who were villains? I mean, magicians are still humans, and humans can be good and evil. Therefore, it stood to reason that a magician could be evil.

Yet I found nothing on that, or any dark forces. And it frustrated me to no end!

But then, with a little help, I made a breakthrough.

Chapter 7

Studying for as long as he did was starting to take a toll on Simon's mind. He was reading without break, putting aside normal sleeping hours and even classwork. Yesterday, he failed a practical exam by failing to form an illusion of different animals in class. Of course, animals were one of the second most difficult visible illusions to form, right behind humans. It involved forming visual and audible illusions together at the same time. He was much more proficient when it came to inanimate illusions, as well as a simple invisibility spell.

Simon was exhausted, with dark bags under his eyes. Yet, with a yawn, he pressed on, and pushed aside another book with no lead to pull out a new one. His body clock was out of commission, but with how empty the library was, he could only assume that everyone was likely asleep. There was a curfew, but professors seemed to give some leniency to students hard at work studying.

Simon opened another journal reflecting on the tales of Edwin the Expressive, a magician originating from Europe in the 1500's. He flipped through the pages but was disappointed to find that Edwin expressed himself through art rather than words. He flipped through the various drawings, but without any words, he could not hope to identify who Virgil the Damned was.

After flipping through the pages, Simon's mind quickly registered something. He flipped a couple of pages back to find a certain drawing. In it, there was a battle between an unidentified magician and a giant lizard (not a dragon since it didn't have wings). His eyes were drawn to the magician, who wore dark red robes and had long gray hair. Simon focused on the magician's face and noticed that his eyes were yellow.

"Archmage?"

This certainly added more to the mystery. There was no doubt about who the magician was. In the present, his hair was shorter and slicker rather than long and flowing, and he wore a coat over robes, but it was still him. What exactly was Archmage doing in the 16th century (aside from fighting not-dragons)? More importantly, how was he so far in the past to begin with.

The library door creaked open. Simon ripped the page off the journal and quickly pocketed it. He did not want to lose this lead, and books in the library exchanged owners each day. Thankfully, they weren't original copies, so it wasn't like he just purposely destroyed an ancient text. He closed the book to hide his theft.

Thankfully for Simon, Morgan entered the library instead of a professor.

"I never took you for a bookworm, Simon," Morgan smiled and walked up to the table.

"I'm really not," Simon yawned out. "I'm just trying to figure something out, but I don't think any of the books here cover what I need."

"I always had a feeling that there was some form of censorship going on," Morgan sat across from Simon. "I mean, do we ever hear about anything bad from past magicians?"

"I've been having those same thoughts. But where would all of those records be? I doubt that they would get rid of them."

"Well, there's one obvious place where they could be."

Simon and Morgan both turned their heads to face the door. Not a whole lot of students would be interested in outdated textbooks, making that the door the perfect hiding spot for any secrets. That's where he would find his answers on who Virgil the Damned was. The two looked back at each other, nodded, then stood up to walk over to the door. Simon tried to open it, but as told, it was locked.

"I can't get it open," Simon sighed out in defeat.

"Well, do you have any lockpicks?" Morgan asked. "For any magic tricks, I mean. A bobby pin would work too."

"I don't. How about a spell? I've seen Archmage open doors with magic."

"Sounds like a plan. How about you make an illusion of an open door?" Morgan smirked.

"I could, but why not enchant the door to open itself?" Simon playfully shot back.

"Point is, neither of us can get this door unlocked with our magic," Morgan shrugged.

"And what are you two doing?"

Simon and Morgan turned back to the library entrance. While they had their backs turned and were busy talking, they had failed to notice that Phoenix was now present. Even though Simon thought they were friends, that wouldn't help them. He knew that Phoenix followed the rules and would not risk getting into any trouble. In fact, he might just try to stop them or report their actions to Archmage.

"Phoenix, my good friend!" Simon greeted. "Morgan and I are having a competition to determine the superior field of magic by opening this door. Would you care to represent the school of combative magic by blasting open this door?"

"No," Phoenix sternly said, arms crossed as he closed the distance between them.

"Did you really think that was going to work?" Morgan glanced over to Simon.

"Not really, no."

"You two are up to no good," Phoenix muttered quietly. "Leave now. I don't want to get you two in trouble."

"But Phoenix--" Simon tried to argue.

"No, Simon. Leave now while you're not in trouble."

"You tried it your way, I'll try it my way now," Morgan grinned.

Morgan stepped forward and locked eyes with Phoenix. There was a moment of silence between them. Simon noticed that Phoenix's eyes started to dilate. Morgan stepped out of the way of the door when he raised a hand towards it. Before their eyes, a bolt of fire slammed into the door, blasting it off its hinges. Afterwards, Morgan snapped her fingers, and Phoenix collapsed, snoring loudly.

"What just happened?" Simon asked. "I mean, aside from that display of magic?"

"I charmed him with magic," Morgan revealed. "I had him destroy the door for us, and then, I had him fall asleep while he was under my control."

"That's actually a good idea."

"And it also means that enchantment beats illusions when it comes to opening a door," Morgan giggled.

"You can brag about it later," Simon stepped into the room. "Come on. I need to find something on Virgil the Damned, and I need as many eyes as I can get."

"Sure thing!"

Behind the (destroyed) locked door was a smaller library. There were small bookcases but no tables. Simon and Morgan looked at different cases, scanning the spines for titles. And of course, Phoenix was right. There were outdated textbooks on all schools of magic. Simon breathed out a sigh, realizing he was now going to get in trouble with nothing to gain from it.

Then, his eyes settled on a word on one of the outdated textbooks.

"*The Study and Application of the School of Necromancy,*" Simon whispered.

Simon instinctively took a step back from the book. He never heard of necromancy while studying at the North American Academy. Yet, the word did stick out to him. He knew that it involved raising the dead, or at least, that's what he remembered. It was likely a form of dark magic. And it was taught to students in this very school. That did not sit well with Simon.

"Simon!" Morgan moved around a case, holding an open book. "I found something on Virgil the Damned!"

"You did?" Simon quickly ran up to her, forgetting all about necromancy. "What about him?"

"He was a magician who practiced dark magic centuries ago," Morgan read directly from the book. "He fought against someone and died. That's it."

"That's it?!"

"That's the gist of it. This book just summarizes the deaths of magicians who practiced dark magic."

"Does it mention anything about his house?"

"Nothing on that."

"I am not having this turn into a dead end. Does it say who killed him at least?"

"Uh, I think it did. Here it is. Killed by Santiago Salvador."

Santiago Salvador has been credited as the founder of Santiago's Shield, although most of his stories are more folk tales than facts. Simon didn't even believe there was actual evidence that indicated he was real. Until now, at least. Finally, he had a clue to go on.

"Phoenix?!" A deep voice called out towards the direction of the blasted down door. "Phoenix!"

"And that's our cue to leave," Morgan said with a worried look on her face.

"That's your cue to leave," Simon took the book from her hands. "I'm not done here yet."

"Simon, we can come back later. If we don't get expelled."

"I won't get expelled with Archmage's sponsorship," Simon grinned. "And I want you to remember that on this day, illusions triumphed over enchantments."

With a snap of his fingers, Morgan disappeared. Of course, she was still there, just invisible. That was a fun spell to play with, Simon thought. He felt her hand briefly touch his, and then, she was gone. Phoenix was going to tell on her, but at the very least, he helped her avoid direct confrontation.

Still holding onto the book, Simon rushed over to the textbooks. Footsteps coming his way, so he had to act fast. He pulled a textbook from the shelf and checked the index. He flipped over to the pages he wanted, and just as he did before, tore them out. He pocketed the papers with the Archmage drawing and put the textbook back in the bookcase.

Simon stepped out of the room, hands up in the air. Phoenix was still on the ground, although he was now waking up. Standing in front of him was someone who looked like an older Phoenix with a bulky build. Although he was bald, he had on an orange coat, green eyes, and furious expression. Simon was slightly afraid to see the man. His fury reminded him of Zack, but the big difference was that this man could use both magic and strength best to knock someone out with a punch.

"Professor Brenton?" Simon greeted hesitantly. "That's who you are, right? Phoenix's uncle?"

"That's me," Professor Brenton stepped forward and snatched the book from Simon's hands. "I don't even know what you did to Phoenix, but you definitely have detention for at least a month. I'll be sure to pass that along to Professor Murdoch."

"Is that really necessary for my first-time offense?"

"Your room. Now." Simon grew more afraid at Professor Brenton's order. "Maybe once I find out what else you do, there'll be more punishments."

"Right. I'll be off."

Simon walked calmly out of the library. When he was finally out of sight of Professor Brenton, he dashed away towards his room. Were all powerful magicians intimidating like him and Archmage? Still, that didn't matter. What did matter was that he had his next lead to pursue and that he had the means to pursue it outside of the library.

Simon opened his room to find Alvin awake and studying. His roommate was more active when everyone else was asleep. He walked over to his own desk and pulled out the papers he stole from the textbook. This was going to help him find out who Virgil the Damned was.

"You're up late," Alvin noted and turned around to face Simon. "What do you have there?"

"This," Simon held up the papers with a grin. "Displacement notes. Specifically on teleportation."

"I already don't like the sound of this."

"This is going to be the start of something new, my friend!"

Alvin sighed and turned back to his notes, shaking his head.

I bet you thought that I was stealing from the necromancy textbook. Unfortunately, Simon the Necromancer doesn't have the same ring as THE STYLISH SIMON, so that was never going to be an option. Instead, I took the chance to grab something from displacement instead.

Why did I take something from teleportation over, say, conjuring animals, which would be a cool magic trick? To start off, if I could conjure up animals, that would make my animal illusions irrelevant (why make a fake when you can have the real thing?). I wasn't thinking about my future as a street performer, but rather, how I would pursue the lead on Virgil the Damned.

And my only lead on Virgil was Santiago Salvador.

I was unlikely to find Salvador's name, or at least, anything revolving around his battle with Virgil, in the library (and I had no intention of going back there anyways). Yet, he was a legend back home in Santiago's Shield. I had to get back home and Archmage made it very clear that wasn't an option.

My theory is that Archmage used displacement to teleport us from Santiago's Shield to the North American Academy. That was how I was going to get back home.

I studied for over a month. This time, it was much more entertaining.

Teleportation is divided into two parts: short range and long range. I practiced short range teleportation as often as I could. When I was alone in my room (or with my confidant, Alvin), I worked on teleporting from one end of the room to the other. It took me a couple of days, but after I made my first successful teleportation, it became a lot easier.

I was building up my courage for long range teleportation with my practice. In bolded letters, the pages warned that someone untrained in long range teleportation could end up in lethal danger. I only had one shot to get to Santiago's Shield and back to the North American Academy safely, and I had to make it count.

While I practiced short range teleportation, I studied long term teleportation with Alvin and Morgan (at the time, Phoenix and I were not on speaking terms). With their help, I would be able to find the safest way back home.

Getting back to the academy would be easy. I just had to draw a teleportation circle in the academy and memorize how it looked. And that's exactly what I drew underneath my bed, for no one to find.

Once I found a way to teleport to Santiago's Shield safely, I would finally be home.

Chapter 8

Simon re-read the notes he had written from the displacement pages while in detention. Thankfully, it was his last day of punishment, meaning he would be free soon. Free from both the classroom and from the academy. If this theory was correct, he would be able to teleport back to his house in Santiago's Shield safely. If so, he would be able to go today.

Cassandra sat at her desk, idly reading a book. Although she was disappointed to hear her student receiving detention, she gave him some amount of freedom in her classroom to practice spells and study. Whenever she tried to catch a peek at his notes, Simon would cast an illusion over the paper to keep it hidden. He did not want anyone to find out his plans before they happened. Although, he had a feeling that the master of illusions could see through his illusions.

"You can leave now," Cassandra told Simon. "You've done your time."

"Thanks!" Simon shot up from his seat and darted for the door.

Simon was quick on his feet with his notes clutched in one hand. He was ready to go back to Santiago's Shield. First, he had to find Morgan. With it being evening, he checked the cafeteria first. There were students finishing dinner, Morgan being among them. He took a seat next to her, unable to hide his excitement with his grin.

"I think I found a way for it to work," Simon whispered.

"You did?" Morgan gasped.

"Come on. I'll tell you when no one's around."

Morgan took Simon's hand firmly and they stood up together. They ran away, with Simon having a slight lead on Morgan. He was thankful that she could not see him blushing. He started to believe that their playful flirting would turn into something more. He appreciated that Morgan was following him despite the danger. She and Alvin were caught up on the story of Virgil the Damned and the reason why they have to get to Santiago's Shield. Alvin was a good friend, but Simon hoped for more with Morgan.

The two arrived at his room. Alvin was asleep in his bed, asleep. With help from Morgan, Simon pushed his bed off towards the side. Underneath it was the ritual circle they drew in white chalk. It was a simple pattern, one that he was able to dedicate to his memory. This was his ticket back to school.

"The house of Virgil the Damned is in jeopardy," Alvin muttered in his sleep.

"Does he do that often?" Morgan asked.

"A lot," Simon nodded.

"The forgotten child will see that the house is secured."

Simon turned his head to Alvin in shock. That was a new line from Alvin's sleep divination. What could he possibly mean by a forgotten child? By secured, did he mean to keep the house safe or take it for themselves? Simon wasn't sure which option was the better one. Slowly, Alvin opened his eyes, and sat up. He stretched his arms with a loud yawn, then looked at his confused friends.

"Were you two watching me sleep?" Alvin asked.

"Should we tell him?" Morgan asked.

"Tell me what?"

"He won't know anything," Simon answered. "We'll worry about that clue later. Alvin, I found a way back home!"

"Congratulations," Alvin said dryly.

"You still need to tell us," Morgan pointed out.

"Of course!" Simon walked over to his bed. "Watson the Wanderer gave two theories for a guaranteed safe teleport. Watson's first theory is the well-known teleportation circle theory, which has been proven time and time again."

"We all know that," Morgan reminded him.

"And his second, less known theory, is that if you hold an object that originated from that household, you can teleport there safely," Simon continued, reaching his hand into his pillow. "This has been proven to be reliable, as long as it has been less than two months since the object has left the destination."

"And do you have an object like that?" Morgan asked.

"I do."

Simon pulled out the birthday card signed by his family from his pillow. He kept it as a memento of his family all this time, and now, it would help him get home. It had been less than two months since he received that letter, so it would grant him safe passageway. He smirked, realizing that despite wanting him to continue his studies, Archmage made his escape possible.

"That's amazing!" Morgan clapped her hands together. "Nothing can stop us now!"

"Alvin, get the ritual chalk!" Simon directed. "I'll draw a circle at my house to make sure I always have a way back there."

"Right," Alvin got off the bed to pull some white chalk from underneath his bed.

"Now, I only need to know where my house is. I can teleport all three of us there safely if I concentrate hard enough."

"Simon, as much as I want to go and meet your family, I can't," Morgan sighed. "I have detention with Professor King coming up."

Of course. How could Simon forget? Phoenix was aware that Morgan charmed him and reported it as soon as he could. Unlike Simon, Morgan assaulted a fellow student with her magic. Professor Brenton called for her expulsion, but ultimately, Archmage decided to give her a final chance and gave her detention for the rest of the year. It was better that she stayed behind anyways. He would not forgive himself if someone got in trouble because of his stunts.

"Of course, Morgan," Simon nodded. "We have to go tonight. Our time is running out. Alvin, you're still coming with me, right?"

"Not like I'm going to be able to get back to sleep anyways."

"Good luck, you two," Morgan gave one final smile, then walked out of the room.

"Congratulations, Alvin," Simon clasped his roommate on the shoulder. "You've been promoted from third wheel to action partner."

"Yay..."

Simon held on tightly to Alvin's shoulder with one hand, and with his other hand, the birthday card. He concentrated, thinking of his home, and his parents and siblings. He focused on those thoughts and willed himself to his room. In doing so, his thoughts turned to his room.

Living space was tight, so he shared a room with Scott and Seth. They both had a small twin bed next to each other, while Simon had a futon. They shared a small closet for all of their clothes. There was a window that looked out to a side street. The lights were usually off in their room, as they did not have light bulbs all the time.

Simon and Alvin now stood in that room.

And sitting on the futon was a teenage couple, who Simon had never seen before, too busy making out to notice the sudden teleportation.

"Cool place," Alvin noted.

"Get off of that!" Simon shouted at the couple. "Get out of here! You're not allowed here!"

The couple looked oddly at the two, then they got up and left, leaving some distasteful words behind. Rock music was blasting throughout the house. Simon took a glimpse through the window to see the neighbor's house. It was decorated with skeletons and jack-o-lanterns. There were children in costumes roaming the streets.

Halloween. One of Simon's favorite holidays. Both of his parents took off work that night to take their children trick-or-treating. Simon used to stay at home with Scott to give out candy to any other children who knocked on their door. But if he was gone from home, and if Scott was too old for trick-or-treating...

"Damn it, Scottie," Simon cursed. "Come on, Alvin. We have a party to stop."

"And not crash the party?"

The duo made their way out of the bedroom and towards the living room, the source of rock music. Simon passed by several teenagers on his way there, with drinks in their hands. He started to recognize a few of them from Zack's gang. This was what he was afraid of if he left Scott alone, without his influence. It was time to put an end to the party.

Most of the teenagers had gathered in the living room, with a new boombox pumping out rock music. Walking over to it, Simon saw Scott and glared at him. His younger brother, talking to two friends, looked away from his gaze. Simon grunted and turned the music off.

A chorus of groans came from the teenagers.

"The fun's over!" Simon declared. "Go on and get out! Whoever brought this boombox, take it with you."

"I don't like you touching my stuff, Simon," Zack, previously hidden from the chair he sat on, stood up. He tossed his red cup aside and cracked his knuckles.

"Just my luck," Simon sighed. "Zack, I don't have time for you right now."

"Then get out of my party."

"This is my house."

"My party."

Simon sighed and grabbed the boombox. "Zack, I really don't want to hurt you."

"Then put my boombox back down."

"You know what?" Simon smirked and said, "I think I can make time for you," just like Archmage said it a few months back.

Zack grinned, ready for a fight. Unfortunately for him, Simon had changed over the past two months. Although his experience with magic was slim, it was enough to give him the edge over the mindless brute before him.

Simon focused, and within that moment, an illusion of himself charged forward at Zack. It was a terrible illusion, but it got the job done. Zack punched the illusion only for his fist to sail through its face. He was confused, giving Simon time to use a short-range teleport to get behind him. Still holding onto the boombox, he swung it over to the side of his head. Zack Attack went down, groaning in pain, before falling unconscious.

"Everyone, leave," Simon repeated. "Someone get Zack too."

The teenagers started to pack up, although they left a mess in their wake. Two of the bigger teens picked up their leader and walked out of the house. Simon passed Zack's boombox towards one of his friends. He noticed that Scott tried to follow the crowd, but Simon teleported in front of him, stopping him in his tracks.

"Simon, how did you do that?" Scott asked.

"Magic, Scottie," Simon smirked. "And it's going to take magic for you to clean up your mess before our parents get home."

"I don't have to clean up anything."

"Scottie…"

"Don't call me that!"

"Oh come on! Your dumb friends aren't even around!"

"Don't call them dumb!"

Simon sighed. "You're right. I can't have you clean up."

"Thank you," Simon grinned.

"Alvin, you have the drawing with the chalk, right?" Simon asked.

"I do." Alvin held it up.

"Draw it in the attic, and then clean up around the house."

"And just like that, I'm now the cleaning service," Alvin groaned but walked off to do his job.

"What are you doing?" Scott asked, slightly worried.

"I'll tell you, after I catch you up on what I've been up to," Simon grinned. "Grab your jacket. We're leaving."

Have you ever lied to someone and they hold it against you for the rest of your life? That's exactly what happened with Scott and me.

Scott used to be one of my biggest fans. He believed that I was magical. Then, he caught a good look at all of my supplies, and that belief just went poof. It's like telling a child that Santa or the Tooth Fairy isn't real (I can already see the hate letters from parents about that line). And he blamed me for destroying magic.

I mean, yes, I did lead him on, and was fully aware that magic wasn't real (or at least, my magic wasn't real) but most people already know that it is fake. How is it my fault that he believed so much in the lie?

That's what I tell myself whenever I think that it was my fault for our bond being destroyed. And, in all honesty, it really was my fault. A simple white lie may be innocent, but it may hurt so many if the truth is found out. So, do yourself a favor, and be honest.

I am thankful that Scott never told the little ones that I was a fraud. I guess that he didn't want to break their innocent hearts. Still, he never got along with me. He pushed me away for years. I don't blame him, but little did he know that it was tearing me up on the inside.

But now, I had a second chance to make things better. I had a second chance to make Scott a believer in magic, real magic, again. I wasn't going to waste that chance. Not when it meant fixing everything I ruined with him.

I told him pieces of where I have been over the last two months. This was all while preparing for my task to track down Virgil the Damned. I decided that if he was killed by our supposed founder, he had to have a grave somewhere in the city. So, first, we had to find where the oldest graveyard was.

Once we found it, we were off to the Santiago Mausoleum, late at night.

Now, at this point, you're probably thinking of how terrible of an idea it is to go to a graveyard on Halloween night, and that's true even without the magic. I want to say that nothing scary happened and that it was a complete success.

But I would be lying if I said that, and I'm trying to lie a little less lately.

Chapter 9

"I'm not buying any of that," Scott declared after Simon finally finished his story.

"Oh come on!" Simon exclaimed.

The two were in the graveyard surrounding Santiago Mausoleum. With a flashlight, Scott shined a light on the tombstones, showing the names. Nothing on Virgil yet, and it was quite an extensive search on top of that. The moon was up high, and it was dark as they walked between the grass isles. Yet, they kept walking in search of Virgil's grave.

During their adventure, Simon recounted his story. He started from when he first met Archmage to his arrival at the North American Academy. He told his brother about the lessons he learned under Cassandra. Then, he went on to explain the friends he met, describing Alvin, Phoenix, and Morgan in detail. Finally, he told him how he came upon his new lead, including his arrival.

And yet, Scott didn't believe him.

"It's just too ridiculous!"

"Alright, I can agree with you on how ridiculous a lot of it sounds, but it's all true, I swear!"

"Magic isn't real, Simon." Scott grumbled.

"Watch this!"

Simon took off his hat and held it up for Scott to see. His brother shined the flashlight over the hat. The magician waved a hand over the hat, forming an illusion of a white rabbit climbing out. He quickly moved his hand through the illusion, showing that it wasn't really there. The rabbit disappeared afterwards.

"You're improving on your routine," Scott noted. "You're finally adding technology to it."

"There is absolutely nothing in my hat!" Simon held it out for Scott. "Go ahead and check!"

"I don't need to," Scott turned his back on Simon, looking at another tombstone. "I know who you are."

"Then explain how I was able to knock out Zack!" Simon argued. "I was in one place, and then I was somewhere else. What happened then?"

"I don't know!" Scott shouted. "Could you please shut up about magic for one minute? It's really all you do, and it gets so annoying!"

"Scottie…"

"Don't call me that," Scott grumbled. "I'm not a kid anymore. I don't need you to look out for me."

"But you do! You threw a party with Zack of all people! At our own house!"

"And now, you have a complete stranger picking up the mess."

"I told you that he's my roommate."

"Sure he is. Look, I want to make my own choices. Zack's a little rough around the edges, but once you get to know him, he's just misunderstood. The same goes for everyone else I hang out with."

"And now you're defending Zack."

Simon sighed out in defeat. There was no reasoning with Scott and his friendship with Zack. There was no way that was a healthy relationship, and he knew a thing about good friends. Morgan and Alvin were both loyal enough to risk breaking the rules to get him back home. And despite Phoenix turning on him, he thought that his fellow magician was a reliable and steady source. Zack was nothing more than a bully.

"I did tell you about how he and his gang attacked me before Archmage saved me, right?" Simon asked.

"You did, and despite the fact that you said time was broken, I believe you on that," Scott shrugged, scanning the last few graveyards.

"And would you believe me if I told you that wasn't the first time he attacked me?"

"Zack told me about that."

"He did?"

"He did."

"And you still hang out with him?"

"I do."

"And you support him?"

Scott was silent for a moment and stopped in his tracks. "Last grave. No Virgil."

"You didn't answer my question."

"You wouldn't like the answer."

"Right. Don't answer me then."

"No. Maybe this will help you, but I hate how you still lie to people with magic. It's wrong. I didn't like the idea that Zack attacks you while you perform, but I won't stop him. Maybe it'll convince you to grow up."

That certainly stung, Simon thought. He was starting to realize that it was a bad idea to drag his brother out to the graveyard. Despite hoping to persuade him back to his side, Scott made it clear that he was firmly on Zack Attack's gang. Even when he showed him what real magic was, he did not buy it.

Then, it hit him. Simon had diverted all of his attention onto magic, both real and fake. It was nothing Scott was interested in. That's what he meant when he said that he grew up. Simon slapped his hand on his forehead. It took him this long to see it, and now, it was too late to apologize.

Simon turned his head towards the mausoleum, built on a hilltop. He took a few steps towards it, and then, an idea popped in his head. In a way, a mausoleum could house Virgil's tomb. The house of Virgil the Damned is in jeopardy. If this was it, how was it in jeopardy? Was what he was about to do going to put it in jeopardy? And who was the forgotten child?

Something extremely cold slammed into Simon's chest and sent him crashing down on a tombstone ten feet away from him.

"SIMON!" Scott exclaimed.

Simon sat up, seeing Scott running up to him. And behind him was someone wearing a black robe and white mask that completely concealed their face. Simon slowly stood up when they started to advance. Of course, given his luck recently, he just had to be thrown in a horror slasher film (with magic). There was a blue flame extending from their hand. The same kind of fire that struck him and stained his coat.

"Scottie, get out of here," Simon told his brother and unbuttoned his trench coat. "Get to Alvin and tell him what happened here. He can tell someone about this."

"But what about you?"

"Honestly, I want to run too, but I have a feeling he won't let me."

In response, the figure conjured a blue flame in their other hand.

"I thought so. Now go."

Simon snapped his fingers to turn Scott invisible. He started to pull off his coat and prayed that his brother ran. The magic the masked magician used was definitely not combative magic. It had to be necromancy. While illusions and displacement aren't considered offensive magic, he had a clever mind to use his new tricks with. This was his fight.

The masked magician tossed the two blue flames towards Simon. He threw his coat in front of him to take the assault, and teleported while he was hidden. Now, he was behind his opponent, and threw a punch aimed at their spine. The stranger fell forward onto the grass, and their white mask turned to face Simon.

Although Simon had magical training, he grew up on the streets of Santiago's Shield. When it came down to it, he could defend himself with his fists. The masked magician threw an awkward blue fireball at Simon while standing up.. He veered to the side to avoid it, then punched his assailant in the gut. They hunched over for a brief moment, then charged forward. They grabbed Simon by the arms, and that's when he started to scream in pain.

Simon could feel powerful magic at work. The masked magician was starting to drain him of something from his body. His soul? His life force? Whatever it was, he realized that he needed it, and without it, he was definitely dying. His muscles grew weaker and he realized it became harder to stand as the spell continued. The masked magician leaned forward, the black eyes on its white mask looking blankly at him as he gritted his teeth to stop his screaming.

Simon leaned his head back and brought it forward rapidly. His forehead slammed into the mask, and there was a cracking noise. The masked magician released him and fell down to the ground a few feet away from Simon. He glanced down and saw half of the magician's mask had fallen off, shattered. He grinned victoriously. It was time to finish them off and find out who attacked him.

After taking one step forward, Simon fell sideways onto the ground.

The draining spell took a toll on Simon's strength and stamina. He was no longer in pain but was very much exhausted. His muscles couldn't even move. For a moment, he tried to concentrate to teleport away, but his vision turned blurry when he did so. He took a deep breath and his vision restored itself.

The masked magician stood up. Simon had hoped to catch a look at their face, but they were careful to cover up what was left of their mask with an arm. With a free hand, the magician conjured another blue flame, readying an execution. Simon tried so hard to move away, but there was nothing more he could do.

Suddenly, there was a flash of lightning behind the masked magician, and Archmage appeared from it.

"This is how it ends for you."

Leave it to Archmage to always save the day. Simon wasn't sure to feel grateful for or tired of his continued insistence at saving his life. The masked magician turned around and took a few steps away. They were covered in blue flames and then vanished. Archmage took a couple of steps forward, towering over the collapsed Simon, analyzing him.

"Was the lightning really necessary?" Simon asked. "Even I thought that was overkill."

"It made for a good bluff."

"A good bluff?"

"It is what it is."

Archmage smirked, then the image started to change. Slowly, Archmage turned into Cassandra, who looked down at him with a frown and her arms crossed. Simon didn't mind being saved by Cassandra. Unlike Archmage, she didn't have a reputation for saving people at the last minute. In fact, he was actually impressed that she saved him in the way she did. He made sure to take notes to try that himself one day.

"Heya professor," Simon tried to sit up but groaned in pain.

"You are going to have so much research on the theory of illusions," Cassandra sighed. "You don't outright fight with illusions. You distract and bluff with them."

"Duly noted. What're you doing here?"

"Archmage asked me to keep an eye on you after your library break-in. Naturally, I did just that and saved your life."

"Thanks for that."

"No problem. Now, I have to get you and Alvin back to the academy. Looks like we'll be opening the medical ward again."

Simon groaned and closed his eyes. After all he went through, he felt even closer to figuring out the mystery of Virgil the Damned. He was attacked while investigating the Santiago Mausoleum. Whatever waited for him there was next in his path. Unfortunately, going back wouldn't be an option for a while.

The North American Academy for Magicians is very unforgiving when it comes to sick leave. I was confined to a bed in the medical ward for a week since I couldn't find the strength to walk. Meanwhile, I was expected to keep up with my education even when I could barely lift my arms. The professors argued that since magic was mental rather than physical, I could keep up with my training. They expected that by the time I was out to pass an exam about what I have learned.

Professor Brenton also gave me another two weeks of detention for breaking curfew and sneaking out of school. That was just twisting the knife.

The worst of it was that as a result of the magical attack I endured, a few stray strands of my black hair turned gray. I did not want to start losing my hair color like that when I was only seventeen. Thankfully, I was able to pluck out a few of the loose strands anyways. Still, the thought of my hair turning gray when I was so young scared me.

Don't judge me. Style is part of my stage name, so I have to care about how I look.

Still, I suppose it was nice to have all of my wonderful friends visit me. Morgan was my most frequent visitor and was intrigued to learn about what happened. She made me promise to have her come with me next time. Alvin also came by and told me that as far as he knew, the teleportation circle he drew in the attic was still intact. That gave us options. Phoenix even stopped by once, and although he didn't say a word, there was a certain fire in his eyes to see what had happened to me.

Cassandra visited when there were no other students to make sure I stayed up on my studies. As promised, we researched theory and practiced animal illusions. Never once did she ask me how I managed to escape from the North American Academy, which had been a question on other professors' minds for quite a while.

"It's always nice to have secrets, Simon. The more tricks you have up your sleeve, the more potential firepower you have in a battle," was all she told me on the matter.

I think even though I was beaten up, she was proud of me as a teacher. Of course, I couldn't help but think about that advice, and how I have never seen her and Archmage in the same room before? Coincidence? Probably.

Speaking of Archmage, he was away on business during my recovery. And when he returned, his first decision was to pull me out of recovery way sooner than expected

Chapter 10

"We have to go back," Simon declared, slowly sitting up on his bed.

"We're going back?" Alvin asked, and Simon nodded. "Did you hit your head during that battle?"

Morgan elbowed Alvin in his ribs in protest, then turned back to Simon with a nod. The trio were alone in the medical wing. It had been closed off due to decline of use and was only reopened after Simon's battle. Many of the beds in the medical wing were worn out, so a new one was granted to accommodate Simon.

With a week to think it over, Simon was now confident that he had to go back and continue with his investigation. He was attacked and left confined to a bed, but he knew he was on the right track. This time, he wouldn't be caught off guard. With all the friends he could get, he was going to get to the bottom of the mystery.

"No one else is doing anything about it," Simon pointed out. "We have to be the ones who do something about it."

"I'm all for it," Morgan said.

"I'm not," Alvin shook his head. "Sorry, but this is getting way too dangerous."

"It isn't that dangerous, Alvin," Simon argued.

"Try to walk without falling down," Alvin countered. "My point is we're not ready to face danger. What do foresight, enchantment, and illusions all have in common?"

"They're fields of magic!" Simon answered with a smile, earning a sigh from Alvin. "Alright. I get it. None of us are exactly magicians suited for combat. So, I thought we would bring Phoenix into our group."

"And there's the first good idea you've had," Alvin faintly smiled at the idea.

Morgan, on the other hand, crossed her arms and frowned. "No. That's a terrible idea."

"Don't worry about it, Morgan," Simon told her. "We need someone who can fight with magic. Phoenix is studying combative magic."

"And do you remember how he tried to stop us before in the library, or did you actually hit your head during that fight?"

"I probably did, but he can fight when we can't. I'm sure that once we tell him how high the stakes are, he'll be interested in joining our cause."

The gates to the medical ward opened. Archmage entered, and immediately, their conversation came to an end. How much had he overheard of their planning? Knowing him, he knew they were plotting before stepping into the room. It was now a matter of what he was going to do to stop them. Simon gulped when Archmage walked towards them. Nothing good was going to come out from this.

"You two are dismissed," Archmage commanded, looking at the two students.

Alvin and Morgan gave curt bows, then walked out of the room. Simon wished he hadn't been sitting up, and instead lying down on the bed. At least then, he could have tried to pretend to be asleep. He was afraid of a punishment from Archmage, remembering his fierce temper from before. Yet, the veteran magician was stoic, as always.

"Mr. Crowley. Come with me." Archmage turned around and walked away.

"Come with you?" Simon leaned towards the edge of his bed.

"You want answers, and I will provide them in my office. Come with me."

"I'm supposed to be resting."

"Not anymore. I'm head of the academy. You're fit enough to return to class. Now, come with me."

"I seriously cannot take ten steps without falling down."

"There is a cane underneath your bed. A blackthorn cane. Consider it a congratulatory gift for your discharge from the medical wing. Come with me."

Simon peeked down, and sure enough, a cane made of black wood was waiting. He was positive that it was not there before, but then remembered that this was a part of who Archmage was (and at least it didn't end up in his hat). He reached down for the cane, as well as his hat by his pillow. After putting his hat on, Simon followed after Archmage, using the cane for support.

After a week in bed, Simon's body still ached from the aftereffects of whatever necromantic spell he endured. Thankfully, with the cane, he was walking, albeit a little slower than before. He lost sight of Archmage quickly but had an idea of where the magician was heading to. The only place they could talk in private was in his office.

Simon did look forward to finding out answers on his mystery. Although it was one of the few secrets that brought out the emotions of Archmage, he had to have answers. Perhaps if he knew what Archmage knew, he and his friends would be able to move forward with that knowledge.

Sure enough, the door to Archmage's office was open. Simon stepped in and took a seat in front of his desk, across from his sponsor. Archmage flicked his hand and the door closed behind him.

"You have certainly proven yourself to be full of surprises, Mr. Crowley," Archmage started.

"What can I say?" Simon smirked. "I needed to pick up surprises when I first started out on the streets. Why stop now?"

"Because it almost got you killed. To be exact, your very life force was drained. It's a miracle you survived."

"It's a miracle that I headbutted my attacker?"

"When one's life is under threat like that, with magic, they lose their willpower. To find the strength to fight back is remarkable."

"And that is why you picked me?"

Archmage paused in deep thought. "One of three, yes."

"Are you finally going to tell me why you picked me then?"

"I suppose I owe you that much."

Simon smiled to himself. One of the greatest questions on his mind was why Archmage sponsored him of all people to attend the North American Academy. It made their random encounter on their first meeting appear to be less than random, as if it was planned. Archmage didn't have to ruin his show, and yet, he did, and it forever changed his life. It was time to finally get answers.

"What's reason two?" Simon asked.

"You have displayed the traits we seek in a student, although perhaps a little too curious at times," Archmage explained. "As I have explained, this academy, and the balance of the world, is in grave danger."

"And you expect me to do something about it?"

"You are already on the right track. For example, you know about the existence of necromancy."

"I've been meaning to ask you about that. Whose bright idea was it to teach students the magic of raising the dead? Isn't that some sort of dark magic?"

"No magic is dark, but rather, the soul of the magician is dark," Archmage said. "And it just so happens that one such magician was the previous professor of necromancy over two decades ago."

"This sounds like the start of a wonderful story," Simon groaned.

"It is what it is."

"So, who are we dealing with here?"

"Darius Murdoch."

Simon paused for a moment. "Any relationship to Cassandra Murdoch?"

"He's her older brother," Archmage revealed. "Two decades ago, two of his students brought a reanimated creature to life. It killed five students. Necromancy was banned afterwards, and Darius didn't take the news well."

"Was I attacked by Darius?" Simon leaned forward, anticipating Archmage's answer.

"Unlikely. If you were, you would be undead, but that's beside the point. Darius took pride in his necromancy as he was descended from one necromancer you have come to know."

"Virgil the Damned," Simon muttered, and Archmage nodded. "It's all coming together. He wants to raise Virgil back."

If it wasn't for how drastic this development turned out to be, Simon would have been happy to have all of his questions answered. Yet, students murdered and a necromancer on the loose was not good news. And whatever Darius had planned certainly was not good news either. Archmage was frightened by the prospect of Virgil's return, indicating just how powerful the ancient necromancer was.

"It is impossible for him to raise Virgil back from the dead," Archmage said in an assuring tone.

"But there was a necromancer at the mausoleum Virgil was buried," Simon pointed out. "The house of Virgil the Damned is in jeopardy. Don't you remember?"

"Although that is where his corpse rests, it isn't his true house."

"Then where, or what, is his true house?"

"You need not concern yourself with these details. Rest assured that it is completely defended. You need to worry about your attacker."

"Not a whole lot I could do regarding that. They got away."

"Mr. Crowley, there is a mole in my academy," Archmage revealed. "Thus, my second reason for sponsoring you. I can trust that you are not the mole, and so, you can find them."

"So, you want me to find the mole that almost killed me?"

"I am confident in your ability to do so."

"Couldn't you just use foresight magic to read everyone's minds?" Simon pointed out.

"I tried, but whoever it is has found a way to protect their mind."

"Of course they did. What about the third reason for why I am here."

"You're not ready for that yet."

"Really?" Simon sighed.

"I suppose I did lead you on there," Archmage stroked his chin. "Ask me any one question, and I will answer it truthfully."

Simon took a moment to think before the question came to him. "How old are you?"

"Fifty-seven."

"Fifty-seven?" That certainly wasn't what Simon expected, from what he read previously.

"Fifty-seven," Archmage confirmed. "You are dismissed, Mr. Crowley."

Simon wanted more answers but the glance from Archmage was all he needed to see. For now, this was all he was going to get, and he was going to have to accept that.

He stood up from the chair and walked out of Archmage's office, cane in hand. It was an exhausting walk to the office, and for once, Simon decided to sleep in his own bed. He started to make his way over to his room when he stopped.

Simon realized that Alvin seemed intent that he did not continue on with his quest. His roommate set him off on his quest with his first dream, but what if it was on purpose? Could Alvin be using him to fulfill some nefarious scheme on behalf of Darius Murdoch? Simon tried to tell himself that couldn't be the case. He trusted Alvin. And it wasn't the only prophecy he gave.

The forgotten child will see that the house is secured.

Simon's thoughts turned towards Cassandra. It seemed very convenient that she showed up when she did to save him from the masked necromancer. Too convenient, he thought. If Darius was descended from Virgil the Damned, and she was his sister, didn't that make her a forgotten child? She went a long way to build trust between her and Simon. It could serve her master plan, the trick up her sleeve.

Suddenly, Simon found it very hard to trust anyone. If the forgotten child is the mole Archmage spoke of, then it could be anyone. He had to be very careful with his next step.

.

Never, ever tell someone that there is a mole in anything unless you have a name, or ways to narrow the list down.

After the conversation with Archmage, I suddenly grew more paranoid. Everyone turned into a potential enemy. I was a paranoid teenager who had no clue who I could trust.

My two main suspects were Alvin and Cassandra.

Alvin's a good man. He's smart in his own way (although a little lazy) and has shown loyalty to not report my schemes to anyone. Yet, he did set me off on this crazy journey with that sleep prophecy he repeated over and over. Additionally, aside from myself and Cassandra, he was the only magician that I knew of in Santiago's Shield. He could have been my attacker.

On the other hand, Cassandra has been my favorite (and only) professor. Yet, she is the sister of Darius, and everything I have seen from her showed that she certainly knew how to deceive someone. It certainly was possible that she was using her illusions to her advantage. In class, while her illusionary Professor Murdoch taught us, I focused on trying to find possible spots where she was hiding, just in case.

And as much as I hate to admit it, the world doesn't revolve around me. It was very much possible that I hadn't even met the mole, who was off running their scheme. Just *like that, I found myself only able to trust a handful of people at the academy.*

I decided that for now, I had to focus on one problem at a time. And despite there being a mole who was actively plotting destruction, I needed to get my body fixed.

So, despite this being a magical school, there's no such thing as a school of healing. I honestly feel like that would have been very useful, especially given that necromantic draining, but not a lot I could really do.

I started to push my body to its limits with simple exercise for a month. I had to get back in shape, and if there wasn't any magic to help, then I would go back to the basics. The workouts did more than help me recover.

Something I learned, asides from alteration and support magic, is that the schools of magic don't help with a physical fight. That gave me an advantage over most other magicians. I wasn't a professional fighter, but you saw how I handled Zack and the masked necromancer. And with the cane Archmage was kind enough to provide me with, I was going to win next time.

After my body healed, it was time to get in touch with the one person I knew I could trust.

Chapter 11

"Phoenix, my good friend!" Simon greeted and took a seat across from him. "How is your day going?"

Phoenix took a glance up from his book, then went back to reading without an answer. The two were in the library, where students were studying for winter exams. Simon was disappointed to have learned that it was a written test on theory rather than a practical one. He was finally starting to get a handle on creating realistic illusions of animals and even humans by now. Theories were so boring to him.

Simon should be studying as well as everyone else, but right now, he had a plot to uncover. His primary concern was finding a close group of friends to help him. Alvin definitely wasn't an option, and although he trusted Morgan, she likely couldn't help in a fight. In the end, Phoenix was the one person who met the criteria of both trustworthy and resourceful.

Simon and Phoenix did not talk much, but based on what he knew, Simon figured that Phoenix definitely had nothing to do with necromancy. His loyalty to the rules was sincere. Additionally, with Professor Brenton as his uncle, Phoenix was unlikely to get away with any spying. Unless his uncle was involved in the plot as well, but the likelihood of that was doubtful.

It was all a matter of convincing Phoenix to join his cause.

"Phoenix, we need to talk," Simon continued on.

"I'm busy studying for my combative exam," Phoenix replied bluntly. "We can talk later."

"I need your help."

"I'm busy studying, Simon."

"You study all the time. There is no way you're going to fail any exam. You're a brilliant student, for crying out loud!"

Phoenix nodded slowly, then glanced up. "Thank you."

"I'm just telling you the truth."

"Then I should do the same," Phoenix smirked. "I don't want to help you."

Phoenix looked back at his book and Simon sighed in disappointment. This was definitely turning harder than he expected it to be. Phoenix held true to his ideals and it didn't help that Simon was a bystander when Morgan used her enchantment magic on him. That destroyed their trust, and although Simon was trying to rebuild that bridge, Phoenix was not interested.

"Phoenix, the entire academy is in danger," Simon continued on, his voice showing his impatience. "The entire world is at stake here."

"Is it really?" Phoenix seemed uninterested. "Or are you being dramatic?"

Simon paused to think. "Alright. Maybe I am being a little dramatic about the entire world part. But the school is in danger."

"How can you be so sure?"

Simon hesitated, then he leaned in and whispered. "Archmage told me so."

Phoenix paused, and slowly looked back up at Simon. "I'm listening. You get one chance to convince me now."

"I really should have started out with that," Simon muttered under his breath. "A student here is not what they appear to be. They are a mole."

"A mole? And who do they work for?"

"Look, I really shouldn't say. Especially not here. People could be listening."

"If you give me a name, and I deem it serious, we may talk in my room," Phoenix offered. "My roommate is currently studying for the support exam. No one will bother us. Or perhaps we should talk with Alvin in your room?"

"Not there!" Simon quickly said. "We'll talk in your room."

"Then convince me or I will return to my studies."

"I don't know if you know this name or not, but Darius Murdoch is the man behind the scenes," Simon finally revealed. "He was a professor here who--"

"I know him." Simon slowly reeled his head back to hear Phoenix's voice with its anger.

"Alright? So, you will help me?"

"Let's talk."

Phoenix didn't bother closing or bringing his book with him. He stood up from his chair and stormed out of the library. Simon was hesitant to follow him. He had never seen his friend break his stoic behavior before. Ultimately, he stood up and followed after Phoenix. His anger showed that he did care about what was happening. All Simon had to do was not paint himself in a bad light and he would have the help he needs.

After a few minutes of walking, Phoenix led the way to his room, across from Simon's room. He opened it and they stepped in. Phoenix and his roommate kept their room tight and neat. The beds were made and the books on each desk were stacked in a presentable manner. It was certainly an improvement from Simon's room. With Alvin sleeping during the day and Simon worrying about the threat of Darius Murdoch, their room had become a complete mess.

"Nice room," Simon complimented.

"Start talking," Phoenix skipped straight to the point. "Don't leave anything out."

"Of course," Simon nervously smiled at Phoenix's furious determination. "Let's start at the beginning then..."

Simon recounted the plot he had become involved in. He started off with Alvin's cryptic sleep messages followed by Archmage's reaction. Then, he told him what really happened during the library visit, followed by the escape to Santiago's Shield. He recounted the battle with the masked necromancer (although made it more impressive than it actually was) and Archmage's reveal of Darius as trying to bring back Virgil the Damned.

Throughout the conversation, Phoenix sat at his desk calmly. It was only when Darius was brought up that his anger returned. He grimaced at the mention of his name and his knuckles turned white. Simon still was not sure how Phoenix knew of Darius, especially since the academy was intent on covering up his presence. Regardless, he had a feeling he found an ally for once.

"And so, you come to me for help?" Phoenix finally asked through gritted teeth.

"I do," Simon nodded slowly. "I really need your help. You're one of the few people I know I can trust."

"Who else do you trust?"

"Morgan, of course," Simon noticed that Phoenix rolled his eyes. "And your uncle. He seems like a good guy."

"Not Archmage?"

"He's not the mole but I definitely don't trust him. Moving on, I don't trust Alvin anymore. There's no way he is accidentally revealing those cryptic messages in his sleep. I don't believe it."

"Wouldn't you know if he was or not?"

"Archmage couldn't find out, but--"

"And a student of foresight is your roommate. It's not uncommon for roommates to learn from each other. I know a handful of support spells myself from my roommate."

"I'm not asking Alvin to teach me. Look, are you in or not?"

Phoenix closed his eyes, thinking to himself. He stood up from his desk and started to pace around his room. His anger had turned quiet, and for a moment, Simon noted that his face was twisted not in fury but sorrow. He exhaled and turned back to answer the question.

"Darius Murdoch killed my parents five years ago," Phoenix muttered.

"Phoenix, I'm sorry," Simon took a step towards Phoenix, reaching out with his hand. "I didn't know."

"That's not exactly a line someone opens with," Phoenix teared up. "They were agents of Archmage outside of the academy sent to deal with villainous magicians. Darius killed them and raised them as undead minions. My uncle had to put them to rest."

"This is getting more and more terrible," Simon placed his hand on Phoenix's shoulder in a comforting manner. "You can stop if you want. I'm sorry for wanting to drag you into this."

"Don't change your mind," Phoenix's eyes snapped open, showing his determination. "I want Darius to pay for what he did. I want to stop his evil schemes once and for all. And you're going to be the way I'll get to do that."

"Let's not get too carried away, buddy," Simon smiled weakly. "We're going to find his mole and stop him from raising Virgil the Damned. I don't think we're ready just yet to directly confront him."

"If I see him, I will fight him," Phoenix declared.

"Look, I ended up on bedrest for a week when I fought his student," Simon pointed out. "If he uses a spell like that, you're going to be nothing but dust. Do you want that?"

"If I see him, I will fight him," Phoenix repeated.

Simon sighed. "Fine, but you're going to follow my lead on how we proceed. No rushing off on your own. Understood?"

"Loud and clear."

Simon was hesitant about bringing Phoenix along. For once, he was throwing logic and rules aside in favor of revenge. It was refreshing to see a new side of Phoenix, but had Simon known what he knows now, he would have never asked him to come along. It may come back to haunt him another time, but for now, he had no choice but to go along with it.

"We need a plan to root out the mole," Simon continued on. "They have to have somewhere to hide while they plot, right?"

"And it can't be in their rooms," Phoenix said. "Their roommate would likely find out if they're hiding anything."

"If only it were that way for Alvin and me," Simon sighed. "So, we need to think of where in the academy they can hide. Do you have any ideas?"

"Couldn't they be outside of the academy? You demonstrated that a student could use displacement to teleport home."

"But how would they get back?" Simon countered, then grinned. "How would they get back? Of course!"

"What is it?" Phoenix raised an eyebrow.

"They need a teleportation circle to get back," Simon started. "We know that they can get to the city, but they need a way to return to school, and that's the only way. We find the teleportation circle; we can cut off their escape."

"You present a good point, and so far, it may be our only clue."

"Phoenix, you know the academy unlike anyone else. Where could someone hide a teleportation circle?"

Phoenix paused a moment to think. "Uncle Solomon mentioned that the academy has a basement. Previously, it was used for necromancy students to practice without ridicule, but it was closed down years ago."

"That's it. Can you find it?"

"Give me time, and I'll try."

"Perfect. I'll catch Morgan up on what happened, and we'll move on."

The two magicians grinned at each other, and after a short farewell, Simon left Phoenix's room. Phoenix was proving to be an excellent addition to a team. Their next stop was the basement. If all went well, they would be one step closer to uncovering who the mole was.

For everyone concerned with Phoenix, you are right to be. He has martyr written all over him, and although I appreciate his drive, there was always the fear in the back of my head that by accepting him to my cause, I was pushing him closer to an early death.

I stand by my decision for two reasons. The first is that even if I rejected Phoenix, he knew everything by that point. There was nothing I could really do to stop him from pursuing Darius on his own. What I could do was help him, guide him to make the right choice, and keep him out of deadly danger. In a way, I was trying to keep Phoenix alive.

The second reason for keeping Phoenix around was that I couldn't do this alone. I tried to do it alone back at the graveyard (sorry Scottie, but you're not a magician like us) and was left broken. I knew I had Morgan's help, but between enchantment, illusions, and displacement, none of us were really magicians suited for combat.

Phoenix definitely was a fighter though. I've seen the power of combative magic when he broke down that door. Magicians who specialized in combative magic were definitely figures of authority when it came to battle. And the fact that he knew how to defend himself with support magic was an added bonus.

So, although Phoenix was definitely walking down a dangerous path, he at least had the right skills to walk down that path.

Time went by as normal. Phoenix was searching for the way to the basement. While he did so, I told Morgan about our new member to the group. She didn't like it at all. It was expected, but there was no turning back. After a short debate (she wanted to keep Phoenix enchanted when we needed him), she decided to trust me.

Afterwards, I continued to practice my physical exercises. I finished recovering for the most part, but I needed my own edge in a battle. Illusions and displacement were a strong pairing, but it needed a little something extra. Combative magic might have been an option, but any magician could account for that. A punch or a cane strike, on the other hand, would definitely be a surprise.

Of course, in doing so, I neglected my studies on the theories of illusions. I ended up failing the winter exam. Cassandra was disappointed with my performance and offered tutoring outside of class. Being prideful, I refused. I knew how to conjure illusions well enough. The theories of their applications were very boring to me.

After the exams, there was a small break for the students, and during that time, my friends and I advanced to the basement.

Chapter 12

Simon wasn't sure why the North American Academy had a winter break for students. They were to remain in the pocket realm during that break, and there wasn't anything to do. The students just remained on campus, ate, and read books. That's all there was to it.

Thankfully, Simon had two friends to help unravel a plot regarding a wicked magician to keep him entertained.

Phoenix had finally found the entrance to the basement. At first, his search came up empty. It was only after he remembered that he had never seen the medical ward because its hallway had been closed off that he started to take a risk and explore the sections that no longer had use. Two days later, walking down one such hallway, he finally found a set of stairs that led downward.

Now, Phoenix led Simon and Morgan through the hallway, which was darker compared to the others thanks to the windows being sealed shut. Thankfully Phoenix held his hand up in the air and emitted a flame from it to guide the way. Simon and Morgan walked side-by-side behind him. The only sound came from Simon's cane tapping on the floor. Finally, the trio arrived at a door at the end of the hallway, one that matched all of the other doors in the classroom.

"This is it," Phoenix glanced over his shoulder.

"Really?" Simon sighed. "I was expecting something, oh, I don't know, a little bit more ominous?"

"Ominous?" Phoenix raised an eyebrow.

"Yeah. This door leads to a basement where necromancy was practiced. I was expecting a big red gateway with runes carved on it that reads 'death awaits' in some ancient language like Latin or something."

"But necromancy itself isn't evil," Morgan pointed out, and Phoenix glared at her.

"My point is that for a magic school, this academy is terrible at decorating," Simon told them.

"I like it," Phoenix told him. "It's almost a second home to me."

"Of course you would think that. Morgan, you can tell me that this looks like a public school, right?"

"Actually, my dad homeschooled me."

"Of course," Simon facepalmed. "Can we both agree that the academy has terrible security? We're about to enter a restricted section and there are no magical alarms going off. I haven't even seen a security camera!"

"Now, I wouldn't say that…" Phoenix quickly turned around.

"I would," Morgan giggled.

"Thank you, Morgan. Now, let's get this semi-exciting adventure over with."

Phoenix pushed the door open to reveal a set of stairs descending down to the basement. The only thing that was even slightly terrifying about the basement was that it was dark. Good thing that they not only had Phoenix to light the way, but also that none of them were afraid of the dark to begin with. The trio pressed on without hesitation, braving the darkness to enter the basement.

Within the basement were hallways, with each side opening up to some sort of laboratory. Simon figured that one was assigned to a student to practice their necromancy on. Simon shuddered at the thought, walking on. It was eerily silent except for the tapping of his cane. Now, unlike the darkness, that was definitely frightening. He gulped, his body going tense.

Simon's mind went back to the night he faced the masked necromancer in the graveyard. Although he tried to laugh it off now, he almost died that night. And now, he was in the supposed lair of his attacker. He glanced over his shoulder, expecting to see the masked figure. Thankfully, there was no attacker. Still, all an attacker would have to do was sneak up on him, and then, that would be the end of him.

Suddenly, Morgan slipped her hand into Simon's and grasped it tightly.

Simon felt his cheeks turn red and was thankful for the darkness to hide them from Morgan. Of course, he wasn't the only one who was scared right now. He had to remain strong for his friends. He gulped down his fears and gave Morgan's hand a reassuring squeeze. Nothing was going to scare him.

A lurching from around the corner caused all three to jump.

"What was that?" Morgan gasped.

"Most likely our mole," Phoenix answered with a flame forming in the palm of his other hand. "Show yourself and surrender!"

"So much for the element of surprise," Simon joked, noticing that his cane hand was trembling.

"We can take whatever comes next," Phoenix declared.

The lurching continued, and as it grew closer, Simon recognized that it was heavy stomping. That couldn't be right. The masked necromancer was a master of stealth, one who walked with grace to sneak up on him in the graveyard. They wouldn't announce their heavy presence.

Simon gagged at the horrid smell, then gasped.

"Morgan," Simon muttered. "Run."

"What?"

The mysterious figure emerged from around the corner and its outline showed it was easily nine feet tall.

"Run!"

Simon pushed Morgan backwards into the hallway and grasped his cane with both hands. Phoenix threw both of his balls of fire at the creature, setting it and its clothes aflame. That did little to stop its slow charge towards them. All it showed was that they were dealing with a stitched-up corpse with rotting gray skin. And it was now on fire too. Simon made a mental note to never complain about how boring something was again.

Phoenix conjured a flame and lightning bolt in separate hands. Simon teleported behind the creature, slightly up from the ground, and slammed his cane towards its neck. It was a beautiful and powerful swing that made direct contact. Simon fell onto the ground, and unfortunately, the creature twisted to turn on him. Simon backed away from the creature's swinging arm to let it slam into the stone wall. The wall cracked from the might of the blow and Simon teleported back next to Phoenix.

"I am not getting close to that thing again," Simon told Phoenix. "That could have taken my head clean off!"

"Then I'll just destroy it on my own!"

With a grunt, Phoenix tossed the bolt of lightning and the fireball at the creature. The fire did nothing, but the lightning caused it to stumble forward. Simon grinned in victory. They finally found a weakness to that monster. Then, it stood up straight, and started to move towards the duo at a faster pace.

"All your spells have done is turn a terrifying monster into a fast and terrifying monster on fire."

"I realize this now. And I don't know a support spell to halt its progress."

"Run?"

"Run."

Simon and Phoenix both started to dash down the hallway, chased by the monster. It was now keeping up a steady pace and kept the two teenagers in its sight. Simon recalled the story of the five students slaughtered by such a creature. He was starting to understand why necromancy was banned. And once they made it to the stairs, everyone else would too once they saw the creature rampaging throughout the academy.

Hopefully, Archmage would stop it before anyone got killed. Although it was starting to get tiresome being saved by Archmage.

Morgan waited by the stairs and looked in terror at the rampaging creature. She pointed one hand out and concentrated. Simon and Phoenix both ran past her and were halfway up the stairs before Simon realized Morgan didn't follow them. He turned back around to go back for her before it was too late.

When he made it back to the bottom of the stairs, Simon was greeted by the sight of the creature standing perfectly still, still on fire, in front of Morgan.

"Morgan," Simon slowly stepped forward to reach for her arm. "What happened?"

"I charmed it with my enchantments," Morgan giggled. "What does that leave the score at?"

"You enchanted an undead monster? Isn't that an inanimate object?"

"I honestly thought so, but then, it worked, so I'll take that."

"What's going on down there?!" Phoenix called from the top of the stairs.

"Morgan stopped the monster!" Simon answered, then turned back to Morgan. "You can just let it burn to ashes, right?"

"I can."

"She's letting it burn! Come on. Let's get back to our search."

Phoenix joined Simon and Morgan down at the bottom of the stairs. The abomination looked ahead blankly while on fire, which was somewhat frightening, but not much so as when it was chasing them. The trio passed by the creature, letting it burn.

Even though he nearly died (Simon hoped this wouldn't become a habit), he pressed on willingly. It was clear to him that the creature wasn't hidden to be unleashed as a weapon. It was there to guard whatever it was the mole wanted to hide. And they were going to find out now what waited for them in the basement.

They came to the end of the hallway, where a room led to a classroom. The desks remained after all this time, although they had been pushed off to the side. In the center of the room was a familiar sight to Simon: a teleportation circle drawn in black chalk. He grinned, taking a few steps to examine it. Phoenix followed after him while Morgan walked to the teacher's desk.

"Can you figure out where this leads to?" Phoenix asked.

"Displacement doesn't work like that," Simon shook his head. "This is an anchor to return to the school. There's not a whole lot I can do to figure out where our mole teleports off to, but we know how they get back to the school."

"Not anymore." Phoenix stomped on the line of the circle and dragged his foot across it, breaking the circle.

"Hey guys!" Morgan called out. "I found a clue."

In one hand, Morgan held a dark robe. In her other was half of a shattered mask.

"That's definitely my attacker's," Simon hesitantly stepped forward. "They're still here and they'll know they need a new teleportation circle."

"They would have known that when they saw their creature burnt to ashes," Phoenix said in a defending tone.

"There's a note in the robes," Morgan revealed, pulling it out from the robes and skimming through the lines. She gasped. "Simon, you'll want to read this."

Simon took the note from Morgan and started to read through it.

Mr. Simon Crowley

You have been quite a thorn in my side. We almost met on that fateful night at the Santiago Mausoleum. My spy had to interfere to stop you in your tracks before you got yourself killed. I thought that their mercy was a sign of weakness on their part due to the attachment you share. Yet, I now hold the belief that you are crucial to my success.

I am close to completing my plan to show the world the true power of necromancy. All I need is the house of my ancestor, Virgil Murdoch the Damned. You will present it to me at your earliest convenience, back at Santiago Mausoleum. In exchange, I will not murder your brother and raise him as my eternal minion. Tell Archmage or a professor, and your family will have one less mouth to feed regardless of what happens.

Respectfully,

Darius Murdoch

"Scottie…"

Just when I thought I was making progress into this plot, something comes up and turns everything around for me.

My first theory on what the house of Virgil the Damned really was did not turn out to be true. Here I thought it was his grave back in Santiago Mausoleum. Yet, if that was the case, then Darius wouldn't demand for the house if he was at the mausoleum. I had no clue about what he wanted from me. Scott's life was in danger all because I couldn't solve a line of a cryptic riddle!

And when I was making progress, it was only because Darius wanted me to get his message. He wanted me to know that he was keeping tabs on me, that he had all of the cards in his hands. I couldn't make a move against him without him knowing. And that was so infuriating!

Darius taunted me with the identity of the mole on top of that. Whoever the mole was, they knew who I was. All I was able to get from the taunting was that whoever the mole was, there was an attachment between us. Whether that is the friendship I had with Alvin or the student and teacher relationship with Cassandra, I had no clue. I was even having my doubts on Phoenix and Morgan.

On the bright side, I could trust just about everyone else in the school.

Yes, I actually thought that. I needed some good news in my life so all the bad news wouldn't bring me down.

I tried not to think about how Scott was a prisoner of Darius. Even today, I try not to think about it. Because it was my fault that he ended up in trouble to begin with. I had to drag him out to the graveyard to prove that magic was real. He knew what I knew, and because of that, he paid for it; it was all my fault.

I love my siblings. I do everything I can to make their lives better. But it was a jerk move to leave them and go with Archmage to learn magic. Scott may have been harsh with his words, but I certainly deserved it. There's more to being a good brother than giving out gifts. A good brother has to be there for their family.

And I was going to be there for my family.

Chapter 13

"Simon," Morgan reached out her hand towards him. "Stay calm."

"He has my brother," Simon's grip on the paper grew tighter to crumple it. "He has my brother and you expect me to be calm!"

"He's right," Phoenix nodded. "We know where Darius is. We take the fight to him now."

"No."

Simon took a step away from Morgan and Phoenix. Anger was taking his mind over. Darius had the audacity to take his brother, hold him hostage, and expected to get away with it. Simon wasn't going to stand for it. Darius was going to pay for his crimes against his family. He already had a plan on how to get to the Santiago Mausoleum.

"No?" Phoenix asked, raising an eyebrow.

"I'm going alone," Simon told them. "Go find Archmage or Professor Brenton. Tell them what we found and do it together."

"Simon, you're going to get killed!" Morgan called out.

"Probably so," Simon shrugged. "Then again, I just have a feeling that something or someone will save me at the last moment."

Simon closed his eyes in concentration. When he opened his eyes, he found himself back in the graveyard surrounding Santiago's Mausoleum.

"Thank you Watson the Wanderer," Simon grinned and released the note from his hands. "Your theories have aided me time and time again."

It was a cold evening in Santiago's Shield. Simon could see his breath and was thankful that the school uniform was thick enough to protect him from the cold. He gripped his cane in both hands and marched uphill, heading towards the mausoleum. He was ready to confront Darius and put an end to his schemes today. No one messes with his family and gets away with it.

When Simon approached the grand doors leading into the mausoleum, he saw a poster on it. Seeing what was on it pushed his anger away.

It was a missing person poster with Scott's picture and description published clearly on it.

Simon realized that Darius was taunting him with the poster, but at the same time, he was thankful for it. Seeing the poster reminded him what was at stake and snapped him back to his senses. This was more than Simon versus Darius, a fight between good and evil. Scott's life was on the line. He needed to be careful. No, he needed to go back and get help. Archmage could freeze time. If anyone could save Scott, it was him.

Simon closed his eyes and concentrated, focusing on the teleportation circle in his room.

When Simon opened his eyes, he was still in front of the poster.

"My bed is over the circle," Simon muttered under his breath. "Damn it."

Simon couldn't afford to wait for help to show up. Scott was in danger, and the longer he waited, the more likely he was to end up an undead monster. He was afraid to face Darius. A master of necromancy could drain away both his life and that of his brothers with a snap of his fingers. Simon had to play it smart if he wanted to escape with his brother alive.

Cassandra's lessons started to pop up in Simon's mind. The theories bore him to no end, but today, they were going to give him the edge he needed. Darius' mole would have noted that he preferred direct confrontation. He had to think as an illusionist for once in his short career as a magician. Simon held his cane in one hand and focused briefly. It was no longer visible, but he still felt the wood in his hands. The secret weapon would only give him one shot. He had to make it count.

With his free hand, Simon pressed the doors open, and stepped closer to danger.

It was completely dark, except for a man holding a torch in one hand, and a knife in another. He was a middle-aged man with white hair who wore a black robe, such as his attacker. But this was someone completely new. Simon let the doors closed behind him and faced the man.

"Welcome to the Santiago Mausoleum," the man greeted.

"Darius Murdoch, I presume?"

"No. I am but Master Murdoch's humble servant, Eustace. Although, I hope that once his plans come to fruition, he will finally teach me his ways."

"You're not a magician?"

"No, but soon, I shall be. Do you have what my master seeks?"

"I don't. I want to talk with him about it."

"You test Master Murdoch's patience, but I shall take you to him, if only for him to put an end to your miserable life."

That certainly was not the welcoming party Simon had been expecting. He cautiously followed Eustace, expecting a trap. The walls were lined with stone coffins of the dead of the past century. Simon was expecting for a skeleton to pop out of one and attack. That thought left his mind. Skeletons were too weak to possibly lift open a stone lid.

Eustace led Simon to a wide chamber where braziers with blue fire lit the room. In the center was an obsidian coffin that was sealed shut. A man stood by the coffin, hand on it. His hair was jet black, just as his trench coat, and his skin was unhealthily pale. He turned towards the sound of footsteps and his green eyes gazed into Simon's eyes.

"Mr. Simon Crowley," the man nodded. "I didn't expect you this early."

"Darius Murdoch?" Simon asked.

"The one and only. You have what I desire, yes?"

"Not quite."

"And you do realize that I have your brother, yes?"

"I have questions. And first off, I want to see my brother to make sure your claims are true."

"Of course. Eustace, get the boy," Darius commanded. Eustace bowed, then walked over to one of the walls to start pulling at a coffin. "Speak your questions."

"First off, you put Scottie in a coffin?!" Simon gasped, his attention on the struggling Eustace.

"There are air holes," Darius assured him. "Now, where is the house of my ancestor."

"Isn't that it?" Simon pointed towards the coffin. "That's where Virgil lies, isn't it?"

"It is where his body rests, but not where his soul is contained," Darius revealed. "Of course. Archmage forbids the teaching of necromancy, even the theories. No wonder you don't know this. But, I am a man of second chances. I will let you leave here alive to bring the house of Virgil's soul to me."

"And do you know where it is?" Simon asked.

"No, and the only one who does is Archmage. Yet, if he sponsored you, he trusts you. He will tell you."

"Boy, you're wrong about that. Archmage really doesn't tell me anything."

"He hasn't told you why he sponsored you, has he?"

"He told me two of three reasons."

"The third is the most important. When next we meet, I want you to know what it is."

"And what would that be?"

"You wouldn't believe me if I told you. Instead, pressure Archmage in telling you. Tell him you walk unless he tells you all of his secrets."

Darius was making a great point, Simon thought. Archmage was asking him to do a lot of work and was secretive behind the reasoning. Darius and Virgil were definitely threats, but Archmage had not answered all of Simon's questions. He wanted to trust Archmage, but that was not a one-way street. It was time for his mentor to show him some trust.

Thud.

Simon and Darius both turned towards Eustace, who had finally pulled the coffin free from the wall. Simon sighed in relief to see the holes on top, as well as the sounds of struggle inside. Scott was still alive. Eustace pushed the lid aside and let it slam to the ground. Scott quickly sat up and tried to make a break for it. However, Eustace was quick to point his knife towards his throat.

"Scottie," Simon called out. "Don't worry. I'm going to get you out of here."

"It sure doesn't look like it," Scott's eyes were focused on his knife.

"We're going to get you home," Simon smiled.

"Once you get me the soul of my master," Darius reminded him. "Now, I am a man of honor. Bring it to me, and you can leave with dear Scottie, unharmed, to return to your family."

"And then we die when you unleash an undead army upon Santiago's Shield."

"I have no intention of doing that. I am simply bringing back my ancestor to remind the world of the power of necromancy. Afterwards, the curriculum at the academy will surely change."

"In any other context, that last line would have been really underwhelming."

"We have a deal, yes?"

Simon would have hated the situation he was in. If he brought Darius the house of Virgil, it would mean betraying Archmage and all of his friends back at the North American Academy for Magicians. Plus, from what he heard, Virgil was not as honorable as Darius. Yet, if he didn't, Scott would die, and his family would be broken from the loss.

Thankfully, Simon had a plan before he stepped in.

"Not yet," Simon declared. "You still haven't shown me my brother."

"What are you going on about," Scott gasped. "I am your brother!"

"So says a possible illusion of my brother," Simon shook his head.

"I assure you that this is no trick," Darius said, frowning.

"Then allow me to touch him," Simon demanded. "That way, I can prove that he isn't an illusion."

There was a short pause from Darius. "Eustace, keep the knife on him, and if he touches for longer than a second, cut him."

Eustace nodded with a grin. Simon frowned, then slowly stepped forward. He was going to get one shot with this. If he slipped up, Scott was gone, and he probably would follow him to whatever afterlife there was. Yet, if he succeeded, Darius would no longer have any leverage over him. His family would be safe, and he would not have to betray any of his friends.

Simon's hand brushed against Scott's cheeks.

Then his invisible cane slammed straight into Eustace's face.

Eustace let out a gasp of pain as he fell down onto the ground. Thankfully, he dropped both his knife and torch.

Simon pressed his hand against Scott's cheek and concentrated. It was now or never. Either his plan worked, or they would die together, and frankly, Simon wasn't ready to die.

Simon closed his eyes, and when he opened them, they were surrounded by darkness.

"Simon?" Scott whispered. "Are we dead? It's so dark."

"We're not dead," Simon quickly hugged Scott. "We're alive. We're alive and in our attic."

Simon put on a strong face throughout the meeting. He had to do so to ensure Scott's safety. Yet, now that it was over, and they were alone, he cried into his brother's shoulder. He would have never forgiven himself if Scott died because he had to involve him in stopping Darius' plot. Scott slowly wrapped his arms around Simon, returning the hug.

Archmage would have to find someone else to stop Darius. Simon was back home, and this time, he was here to stay.

It definitely wasn't an easy choice on my end, but after rescuing Scott, I was very serious about bailing on Archmage and his academy. Call me a quitter. Call me a coward. Call me a drop-out (which was true before today anyways) but I wasn't going back to help deal with Darius.

Something I came to accept was that Archmage was a terrible boss. I guess he's the kind of guy who prefers doing the job himself, but when he can't, he does nothing to help out. I mean, he knew that I investigated Santiago Mausoleum and did nothing about it. If he had been paying attention, I wouldn't have had to risk my life to save my own brother.

I probably was going to have my own regrets regarding my choice. I was definitely going to miss Morgan and Phoenix. I was glad that the academy opened my eyes to what magic was and I was definitely going to miss out on studying at some of the other schools.

Not like I could go back anyways. With my bed over my own teleportation circle, there was no going back unless Alvin decides to move it for no reason. Phoenix and Morgan would probably think I got killed, so I don't think they would help out either.

But, when it came down to it, I didn't want to go back.

The next morning, all of my siblings greeted me. I showed off some of my illusions while we caught up over breakfast. Christmas was coming up, so I had to go out and get presents for them soon. I needed to go back to the streets to perform for money again, but with a few new tricks up my sleeve, that wouldn't be a problem.

I stayed at home with my dad while mom was at work and the others went off to school. It was the last week of school they would have before they got out for winter break. I would have time to pull off new tricks while they were in class, but for now, I needed to rest.

You know, this would be a perfect place to stop writing. We have a happy ending where the hero saves his family and he makes a sacrifice at the end. However, my place in the narrative isn't over just yet.

Chapter 14

Simon carefully took a sip from his hot chocolate, seated by a chair in front of the fake pine tree set up in the living room. Ornaments of all kinds were hung from the branches. Many of the Christmas decorations had been created by his siblings. Some were not great, but it was the thought that counts. It wasn't that long ago when he made his own decorations for any upcoming holiday.

It was early afternoon now and Simon was taking time to relax. He wasn't alone either. His father was over in the kitchen, sipping from a cup of coffee. When Scott went missing, he changed his work schedule to be free during the day to watch over his youngest child, Sara. Even though Simon could have watched over her, he was told that he already had the morning off.

Simon had caught up all of his family on where he had been. Of course, he left out all of the dangerous parts, such as the conflict with Darius. Rather, he focused on the magical aspects and even showed off a few illusions as an example. All of his siblings (except for Scott, who was mostly silent) enjoyed the magic and believed him. His mother also believed him, having seen Archmage's previous gift. Simon thought his father would be the only one to have doubts, but surprisingly, he believed him as well.

"You over-exaggerate a lot, but I have never taken you as a liar before, and I won't now," was all Phillip said on the matter before going back to reading the morning newspaper.

For once, Simon was at peace. He had been worrying over Darius and his secret agent for so long that he forgot how to relax. He was in desperate need of a break, after all he had been through. And this break was going to be a permanent one. He learned enough from the academy. Archmage would have to find a new student to sponsor. It wasn't going to be him. Not anymore.

Simon heard a crashing noise come outside and sighed. At this time, high school released their students. Zack and his gang must have knocked down the trash can again. That would be a minor bump to his break but nothing he could not handle. Thankfully, with his newfound experience, Zack was now the least of his worries. Simon stood up and picked up his cane to walk towards the front door.

When Simon opened the door and stepped outside, he was surprised to see Zack and two of his buddies picking up after the trash. Scott slowly walked to put his bike away by the house, purposely avoiding looking at his brother. Simon took a few hesitant steps forward. Zack turned the can upright, then focused his attention on Simon.

"You're back, huh?" Zack asked.

"I'm back," Simon nodded.

"Good," Zack took a deep breath in, and reached into his back pocket. "Look, man, I've been thinking."

"That's new for you."

"Ha-ha. Very funny," Zack grunted. "Well, I guess I've been talking with your brother for a little, especially after he came back. And, it's hard to say, but I'm sorry."

"Sorry?" Simon raised an eyebrow in surprise.

"Sorry for beating you up and takin' your money," Zack grumbled and took out some money from his pocket. "I… look, man. I don't come from a good family. You do. I didn't like how you were taking money from people and being so generous about it. I think when you beat me up back at Halloween, you used magic, right?"

"I did." Simon took off his hat and held it out towards Zack. There was a moment of hesitation, but ultimately, Zack dropped his spare bills in it.

"I'm changing my ways," Zack admitted. "Still keeping my friends around, but your bro showed me that this path wasn't going to be good for me."

"In jail?" Simon smirked.

"More like on the streets needing money, but unlike you, I don't have a special talent," Zack got back on his bike with his friends. "I'm keeping the gang around, but I'm going to try to graduate next semester."

"That's… that's actually good to hear, Zack."

"Catch you around, Simon."

Zack and his friends rode off down the street, not looking back. Simon was surprised by Zack's turn of redemption. He placed his hat back on his head and turned to face Scott. His brother was by the door, but they locked eyes for a moment. Scott smiled upon seeing Simon's confusion then stepped inside. Simon followed after him, but as he walked up the final step, he felt a breeze come from behind him.

Simon glanced over his shoulder to see Archmage, flanked by Professor Brenton and a woman wearing brown robes.

"Mr. Crowley," Archmage greeted.

"Nope." Simon stepped inside his house and slammed the door shut.

Simon knew that he was only delaying the confrontation, but that one act of protest gave him a spark to fight back. If Archmage had hoped to drag him back to the war, then he had another thing coming. He was not going to leave his family, especially during the holidays. Not after Archmage decided that they were expendable for Darius and not worth the protection.

Simon returned to the living room, where Scott had taken a seat. The two brothers sat in silence, the elder taking another sip from his hot chocolate. The silence was awkward, but it was a step up from Scott running off when they were in the same room. There was a knock on the door. Simon turned towards his brother and shook his head. They remained seated as the knocking continued for several seconds. Ultimately, their father got up from the kitchen to answer it.

"Good day," Simon heard Archmage's voice. "You are currently housing one of my students. I must have a word with him. May I come in?"

"I don't think so. My son told me that you didn't let him come and visit. I'm not sure what else he's hiding, but he's still my boy, so--"

"You will invite me in and return to your business."

"Come on in!"

Simon facepalmed. He was pretty sure it was unethical to use magic to invite yourself into a household like that. But of course, it wasn't like there were any laws stopping mind control with magic. A few seconds later, Archmage entered the living room, alone. Professor Brenton and the woman, presumably Professor Montague, remained outside, standing guard. Now Archmage was worried about protecting the Crowley family.

"Good day, Mr. Crowley," Archmage greeted.

"Get lost," Simon replied back. "You mind controlled my dad with magic. That's almost as bad as necromancy."

"Ah, you say that, but you associate with someone who practices enchantments," Archmage smirked. "It isn't magic that is evil, but rather the magician."

"Should I go?" Scott asked.

"Stay," Simon answered and kept his gaze focused on Archmage. "You use magic on him at all, we're going to have a problem."

"Understood," Archmage sighed. "Teenagers. So much potential, yet so volatile with their emotions."

"Hey!" The Crowley brothers said in unison.

"It is what it is. Now, I suppose you have problems with me. Do you care to share?"

"You mean you haven't read my mind to find out why I'm not coming back?"

"I have. I always think that sharing problems out loud clears the mind. Be honest, Mr. Crowley."

Simon inhaled, then exhaled. "If you insist. You leave me, a teenage boy, to prevent the return of an ancient and evil magician by the hands of his descendant, a former professor at YOUR academy. You tell me that there is a mole but give me no way to find them, leaving me paranoid. You do not care for my wellbeing, or that of my family, at all. Perhaps if you had been there for me at some point, I would be more accepting of you. At this point, all of my suspects for the mole have been of more help than you. So, in conclusion, get out of my house!"

By the end of his rant, Simon was livid and breathing furiously. Yet, throughout all of it, Archmage remained stoic. Scott reclined back into his chair, whistling nervously. Slowly, Simon started to calm down, thanks to the rant and his breathing. He took one final breath in and let it out as a sigh. Archmage proved himself to be right about one thing. That did help.

"As we speak, Professor Montague and Professor Brenton are fortifying your household," Archmage revealed. "I do apologize. I honestly thought Darius would leave your family out of it, especially your brothers and sisters. He hasn't been known to harm children, especially after his child was taken away."

"The forgotten child," Simon muttered. "Archmage, could it be possible that at some point in his life, Darius found his child."

"It is very possible," Archmage nodded.

"That… that has to be his mole then."

"Simon," Scott spoke up, and the two brothers locked eyes. "You have to go back."

"I have to go back?" Simon repeated, confused.

Scott nodded. "I'm scared, Simon. If Darius wins, I don't think any amount of magic will keep our family safe. I can try to do something with Zack and his friends, but if we're being honest, we don't have the training like you and your friends do. Please, Simon, put a stop to Darius."

Slowly, Simon smiled at his brother. That was the first time he heard Scott speak about magic in a positive way. He was no longer the disbeliever that he had grown up to be, and that warmed Simon's heart. It was going to be a hard decision, but if he had Scott's backing, he certainly had the backing of all his family. Simon turned back to Archmage with a sigh.

"I'll go back, but I have two demands," Simon said, holding a single finger up. "You get my brothers and sisters all the Christmas gifts they want."

"It will be done."

Simon held up a second finger. "You will answer all the questions I have. About you. About Virgil the Damned. About me."

This time, Archmage hesitated, but ultimately, he nodded. "Of course."

"Scottie, tell the others I'll be back soon enough," Simon stood up, cane in hand. "And if they ask where I am, tell them I'm on another magical adventure."

"Right," Scott quickly got up from his seat, and the two brothers hugged. "Take care."

"You too."

"Professors Brenton and Montague will follow us after they're done," Archmage told Simon. "Let us be off."

Archmage extended his hand towards Simon.

Simon hesitated this time. He took one final glance towards Scott, gave him a friendly smile, and gripped Archmage's hand. Then, the two were gone from the Crowley household and back at the North American Academy for Magicians, in the same hallway as when they first entered.

"My office, Mr. Crowley. It is time I held up my end of our deal."

What kind of protagonist would I be if I decided to drop out of the story about halfway through the plot anyways?

Now, let's get something out of the way. Once Darius was dealt with, I was going to go back home and never go back to the academy. I mean, magic is cool and all, but I learned all I really wanted to know. I knew how to create illusions straight out of my mind and how to escape danger with a snap of my fingers. I didn't care about controlling people's mind or seeing the future or blasting someone with fire.

If we're being honest, I had no clue what I was going to do with my life. This whole experience was teaching me about how to be responsible for my actions. So, I decided it was time to live as a responsible young adult. Maybe I would get a good entry job or get my GED.

It was a big sacrifice to simply move on from my initial dreams of using my new magic to make a profit. Granted, I probably would be very famous if I did go public, but from the looks of it, the magician community was very secretive. They probably wouldn't appreciate it if some teenage drop-out decided to take their teachings and put them to his use in that manner.

Plus, it seemed like magicians have some way of getting paid. Archmage was loaded and I doubt that the professors were working at the academy out of the goodness of their heart (although it certainly was possible). This probably goes back to the war Archmage spoke of. Boy am I glad that it was going on in the background. If I had gotten involved back then, I would be dead.

With that in mind, I decided to make becoming a star magician my back-up plan.

Don't give me that look. I am allowed to use my magic to make a profit if all else fails. A "break glass in case of emergency" kind of deal.

Still, before I could settle into an early retirement, I had to help Archmage out, one last time. At least he was starting to be more helpful and willing to answer my questions.

I thought a little bit about my strategy on how to proceed. With what I knew, I decided it was time for a change of tactics. Something that no one would expect. I was hesitant to go with it. It certainly wasn't a plan Archmage would approve of.

But after our conversation, I certainly didn't care for what he had in mind.

Chapter 15

Simon ended up in the principal's office more than he thought he would during his time at the academy. Once more, he found himself seated in a comfortable chair in front of Archmage's desk. Archmage himself did not take a seat but was rather looking at his bookcase. He had been silent throughout the hallways, and that silence had persisted even now.

"So, are we going to talk or what?" Simon finally asked.

"In all due time. I wish to show you something that may help you understand the questions you have."

Archmage grabbed hold of a tome with red leather on the top shelf and pulled it. The bookcase swung wide open, revealing a secret chamber. Honestly, after all Simon had seen, a secret chamber with a secret doorway was pretty mundane. Why not put in a magical gateway to a secret room? Still, Simon saw potential with this new secret. He memorized the tome Archmage pulled and followed him inside.

The chamber held all sorts of items within it. Relics, Simon realized. He looked in awe at the sight. Now, this was what made the chamber anything but mundane. The chamber held dozens of valuable artifacts that drew Simon's attention. While Archmage walked to a jar in the back of the room, he quickly looked at as many other artifacts as he could see.

"What's this?" Simon pointed towards a cracked, teal orb on a podium.

"Dwayne the Honest's Orb of Foresight," Archmage answered. "With it, you can view any location that comes to mind."

"Cool," Simon muttered, then turned his gaze towards a dagger sealed in a glass case. "How about that?"

"The Fang of Arachne. Be careful. A single prick will leave you poisoned, and you will find your life sapped away."

"But there's a cure, right?"

"There isn't. A powerful magician such as I may be able to use their power to delay it, but there is no cure."

"Uh, alright," Simon quickly looked at the next relic he could find, which was the jar Archmage walked to. "And that?"

"The phylactery of Virgil the Damned," Archmage said nonchalantly.

"The plylactarwhat?"

"Phylactery. However, given its difficult pronunciation and spelling, many modern magicians simply refer to it as a house, a house for the soul."

Which disgraces the legacy of necromancy.

Simon paused for a moment. "You heard that too, right?"

"Indeed I have. Good day, Virgil. You haven't had the chance to meet him, but this is the student I sponsored, Mr. Simon Crowley."

I would shake your hand, but I lack a body. And even if I did have one, when we shake, I would simply drain your soul and leave you a broken husk.

Simon instinctively took a step away from the jar. There was very little Virgil could do, especially in his given form, but his very presence was a shock to the young magician. A terrifying evil lived to the present day, hiding away within the very academy he thought was secured.

"There is nothing to worry about, Mr. Crowley," Archmage assured. "Virgil is quite powerless in his phylactery. I was never worried about someone stealing him away from me as well, especially Darius."

My descendant will be the end of you.

"The only area in which Darius is better than me is necromancy. I am his superior in every other field."

I wasn't talking about him.

"The forgotten child," Simon muttered. "Archmage, Darius' child is in the school. They're the mole."

No wonder you picked this one. He has potential.

"Potential?" Simon turned to Archmage. "That's what you said, wasn't it?"

"Worry not about his words, Mr. Crowley. That is all he has against us now. Virgil's very soul is trapped within that jar. It will take a ritual to restore him to have a physical form."

"And why not destroy the jar?" Simon pointed out.

"His soul would go free, ready to possess whoever he desires," Archmage answered. "A phylactery has weaknesses set by its creator, and when one acts on the weaknesses, the soul is destroyed as well. Virgil set two weaknesses: he may only be undone by necromancy, and by his own line."

Darius and his brood are too devoted to my cause to destroy me. Meanwhile, Cassandra lacks the will to wield necromancy to begin with. I like my odds.

"Cassandra won't destroy him?" Simon asked in disbelief.

"She is a good woman but is afraid of her legacy," Archmage confirmed. "I have tasked her with the destruction of Virgil before, but she is afraid of what necromancy will turn her into."

She is a disgrace. If I could, I would disown her. But enough about me. I can tell that the boy doesn't know. Do you want to tell him about who you really are?

"That is not important," Archmage shrugged.

"No, it is," Simon started to reach into his trench coat. "I need answers."

"You have your answers."

"Not all of them."

Simon pulled out a piece of parchment from his coat and unfolded it. He held it up for Archmage to see the drawing of himself, straight out of the textbook. Archmage glanced at the picture, and for a brief moment, Simon saw the recognition in his eyes. He knew. Simon let him take the paper from his hand to examine it closely.

Perhaps he should not have pushed someone so powerful for answers. But, if they were going to continue working together, Simon needed to learn more about Archmage. He opened up about the continued existence of Virgil the Damned. This should be no small feat.

"I suppose you are ready, Mr. Crowley," Archmage sighed. "Archmage was not my given name."

"Yeah, duh. No sane parent would want to name their child that."

Archmage chuckled. "Yes, I suppose so."

"Let's just cut to the chase. Tell me that man is you."

"It is me, and it isn't me."

Simon blinked. "I… that's not how that works."

"Magic," Archmage smirked, and Simon facepalmed. "Magicians first started to emerge during the twelfth century, and among them, there was one who was more powerful than the rest. He was the first Archmage."

"So, it's a title passed down?"

"Not quite. Whenever a new Archmage is selected, they sacrifice their name, and their identity, and everything that made them who they were before."

"But why?"

"It makes the transition easier," Archmage took a breath in. "Mr. Crowley, the power of an Archmage is passed down from master to student, ever since the first one."

"Which means that with each generation, the current Archmage is more powerful than the one before him," Simon realized.

"You catch on quick. But more than power is passed on. The memories live on. I remember fighting that wyrm. I remember meeting with kings and generals alike. I remember the wars I fought in, the friends I made, the lovers I had, and the villains I have defeated. And yet, none of them were me."

Simon simply looked on in silence, unable to come up with the words to react. Here he was, learning the secrets of one of the most powerful magicians alive. He saw Archmage truly vulnerable. Not afraid or angered as he was when he discovered the plots running against him but vulnerable. His eyes showed fondness as he embraced the nostalgia.

That was not the only reason why Simon remained silent. Archmage wouldn't trust him with such secrets, even if it was just to gain his trust. No, there was much more to it than that. He hoped that it was not going to end up how he was thinking it would, but Simon could not think of another route this conversation could end up like.

Ultimately, it was Virgil who broke the silence.

Tell him. He already knows.

"There is no going back once I tell him," Archmage muttered.

"Tell me," Simon demanded, his voice rising. "Tell me, damn it!"

"Mr. Crow- Simon, I have seen my own death," Archmage revealed. "I know not what will take me, but my time is growing ever closer. The lineage of the Archmage cannot die with me."

"No..." Simon took a step back, still trying to find a way to reject the truth.

"You've been wondering the third reason why I picked you," Archmage continued. "I want you to replace me."

"No," Simon continued to repeat. "No. No. No."

It was definitely too soon to tell him.

"Mr. Crowley, you remind me of myself when I was your age."

"No."

"You're clever. You think outside of the box. You have challenged death time and time again and managed to escape with your life. Although you may be a little too... exaggerated at times, these are the qualities that would make you a good candidate to be the next Archmage."

"NO!"

Simon's outburst was sudden and silenced Archmage. He was willing to stay long enough to deal with Darius, but now, Archmage was asking too much of him. He was asking for Simon to give up his life and become an all-powerful magician. Although such an idea would be tempting to many, Simon knew better. He was not going to become part of Archmage's collected memories.

"I understand the complaints you have," Archmage spoke up. "A few more years here may help you see the bigger picture."

"I'm not staying here for another few years," Simon told him. "Once we stop Darius, his child, and maybe destroy Virgil--"

What did I ever do to you?

"Shut up, Virgil. Once I'm done solving YOUR problems, I'm going back home."

"Do not be so quick to deny my power. Already, by taking the fight against Darius, you are displaying the traits you need to have."

"Stop your sales pitch. You are asking me to give up my identity. You are asking me to be Archmage, and not Simon Crowley, or the Stylish Simon!"

Does he really go by and call himself that?

"I do and I am proud of it!"

I swear, if Darius loses to someone with that ridiculous of a name, I am disowning him.

"Simon…" Archmage sighed. "Mr. Crowley, feel free to continue on with whatever plans you may have. If you need to talk--"

Simon didn't bother sticking around to listen to Archmage. He stormed out of the secret chamber, and for good measure, closed the bookcase behind him. He was furious at Archmage for picking him to sacrifice his life, his family, his friends and everything to become some sort of powerful guardian. That simply wasn't his kind of style.

With that in mind, Simon was confident in his ability to defeat Darius without the power of Archmage. This time, he was about to prove a new point. Power doesn't win battles. Rather, a cunning mind of a magician can outsmart even the most powerful of foes. That is what he believed in.

And with his newest yet craziest plan, Simon knew that no magician, no matter how powerful they may be, would be able to stop him.

.

I certainly have some choice words to describe Archmage right now.

But seriously. What Archmage tried to pull on me there, the worst decision of his life (or is it lives? I don't know anymore!). Who was he to think that he could make me the most powerful magician on the planet, gifted with the wisdom and experience of all of the predecessors before me?

You know, when I write it like that, it does sound like a sweet deal.

You're all probably thinking why I am so insistent on not taking Archmage up on the path he wants to set me on. Especially when I talked about wanting to be responsible. Taking up guardianship of the world from supernatural evil is a responsible job, sure.

But it wasn't my job.

In any other circumstances, I would have thought that a powerful magician transferring their power to another powerful magician over and over would be a good idea. But when I'm given that choice, I suddenly start thinking about what is at stake. So, before you start to judge me, wait until you're in my shoes before coming to any conclusions. I stand by my choice.

Plus, I wasn't going to give up on my family, ever. Archmage may be able to make that choice, but I guess I'm selfish enough to not make an ultimate sacrifice for the benefit of the world, even my family. Sorry, world. You'll get yourself a new Archmage, but it won't be me."

Anyways, I had bigger problems to worry about, like my endgame plan to defeat Darius once and for all.

Virgil still being around certainly got me thinking. Darius's entire plan to bring necromancy back to the curriculum of the North American Academy for Magicians (still a ridiculous motive, but whatever) relied on bringing Virgil back. However, if there was no Virgil to bring back?

I had a plan.

I have been teasing this plan for a while now. I bet you have been wondering what master plan I have created. You have been on edge just to learn what it is.

You will find out if you keep reading.

Yes, I used that exact same strategy before. I like building suspense, what can I say?

Chapter 16

Simon needed to get the team back together, and the first person to talk to was someone he had been wrong about.

After walking away from Archmage's office, Simon immediately returned to his dorm room. He did not have a lot of time to work with, so he needed to gather all of his friends quickly. Once they were informed and accepting of the crazy idea he had, then the fun could truly begin.

Simon unlocked his door and stepped inside. Given the time of day, Alvin was in his bed, snoring. He sighed to see his roommate like this because for once, he would have to play the villain. Simon clapped his hands loudly, trying to wake Alvin up.

"The house of Virgil the Damned is in jeopardy," Alvin snored.

"Yeah, we've had this conversation before," Simon continued to clap.

"The forgotten child will see that the house is secured."

"Been there, done that. Now, wake up already!"

"The master falls victim protecting his future during the battle."

Simon stopped clapping. "Alright. That's a new one."

"The upcoming battle is only the start of the path the aged magician walks."

Simon facepalmed. Of course, because of his initial distrust of Alvin, he stopped paying attention to him. Now, there were two new lines to the prophecy revolving around Virgil the Damned. To take his time to fully decipher the prophecy could be a waste of time. By the time he solved it, it could be too late. No, he had to go with his plan now. Still, he briefly dwelled on the lines.

The first two lines were obvious by now. Simon focused on the next line. The master falls victim protecting his future during the battle. After a little bit of thought, he settled that Darius was the master. Even Archmage admitted that he was his superior in necromancy. And his future was with Virgil. Well, on the bright side, the evil magicians were going to lose. They had that much going for them.

The last line was very much cryptic. It couldn't mean any middle-aged magician. No, something about being aged made the magician special. Archmage came to mind but there was no way that this was the start of his path. In all honesty, it probably would not play a difference in the battle. Virgil and Darius were going to be defeated. Let the old magician walk whatever path they wanted for all Simon cared.

Alvin yawned and sat up to look at Simon. "Oh. Hey. I haven't seen you in a while."

"Well, that was kind of because I've been trying to avoid you," Simon admitted, rubbing the back of his head awkwardly.

"Why?"

"Well, I thought you were a mole for Darius."

"For who?" Alvin blinked in confusion

"I'll tell you later. But I don't think you're the mole now. You saved my life by drawing that teleportation circle in my attic. If you didn't do that, I wouldn't be here, talking with you."

"Alright. Cool." Alvin shrugged.

Simon smiled. "This is why I like you, Alvin. You care enough about me to follow me, but also not enough to get too mad that I didn't trust you. Now, let's get you caught up."

Simon spent the next few minutes catching Alvin up on the plot, all the way up to his meeting with Archmage. Of course, for his sponsor, he left out the details regarding Archmage's condition, but Alvin knew Virgil lived on. In hindsight, he realized how terrible of an idea it was to turn on his friends because of one mole. From now on, he was going to trust his friends. What were the odds that someone in his close circle of friends was going to betray him? He was too charming to be betrayed.

"I missed out on a lot," Alvin muttered.

"You sure did," Simon grinned. "Stay here. I'll grab Phoenix and Morgan."

Gathering the others was simple. First was Phoenix, who was practically his neighbor. Two knocks later, and he answered (for some reason, he always answered instead of his roommate). Phoenix hugged Simon for being back, then pushed him away for leaving them behind. Simon promised to catch him up once they had Morgan. He didn't want to tell the same story three times.

Thankfully, Phoenix knew a mental messaging spell, and was able to get in touch with Morgan. The duo went over to Simon's room to wait with Alvin for her. After a few minutes, there was a knock, and Simon answered. Morgan immediately tackled him with a hug, worried that he was killed by Darius. After they parted, he caught her and Phoenix up on what they missed. Now, with a few minor exceptions, such as Archmage's secret or Simon's plan, they all knew everything about what had happened.

"Archmage is hiding Virgil the Damned's phylactery in his office?" Phoenix asked once more. He was still trying to wrap up that minor detail.

"It surprises me too, but we can put an end to Darius' plan once and for all," Simon grinned.

"And how are we going to do that?" Alvin yawned. While the others remained standing, he was on his bed.

"Tonight, we're going to steal Virgil from Archmage."

"Count me in!" Morgan said without hesitation.

"And this is when I step out," Phoenix sighed. "We're going to get in a lot of trouble if we do this."

"That's what makes this exciting."

"I still have my objections."

"Of course you do, but you haven't left yet."

Phoenix sighed. "If anything goes wrong, it could mean the end of us. Yet, if it means putting an end to Darius's plans, the risk is acceptable. I'm in."

"Do you really want me?" Alvin asked. "I mean, all I'm good for is seeing the future. And I'm terrible at that too."

"You're one of us, Alvin," Simon smiled. "We need a good lookout."

"Well, I guess I'm in too."

Simon continued to smile brightly at his group of friends. When all was said and done, they would follow him with whatever dangerous and crazy idea he had--from breaking into the restricted section of the library to sneaking out of the academy. To battling an undead monster to stealing one of the most powerful artifacts from one of the most powerful men alive. This was what loyalty looked like.

"So, what's the plan?" Phoenix asked.

"I'm glad you asked!" Simon clapped his hands together. "Alvin will remain here and stand guard over my teleportation circle."

"Easy enough," Alvin agreed.

"Phoenix will stand watch over Archmage's office. If anyone tries to step in after Archmage eventually goes to sleep, he'll distract them."

"Err, alright," Phoenix said, questioningly.

"Morgan and I will sneak into his secret vault and steal Virgil the Damned's placata-"

"Phylactery," Phoenix tried to correct.

"His house," Simon settled. "And then, we will all teleport back to my room."

"Do you know how to get to his vault?" Morgan asked, curious.

"It's behind his bookcase," Simon answered. "We get in with a red spell book on the top shelf."

"And then what?" Phoenix asked. "None of us here are related to Virgil."

"None of us here are, but Cassandra is," Simon pointed out. "She owes me a favor for keeping a certain secret all this time. She just needs to learn one necromancy spell, probably the one with the flames, and destroy Virgil."

"And if she doesn't?" Phoenix continued to question.

"We get expelled. Look, I get it isn't a perfect plan, but go ahead and suggest a new idea? A spy is moving against us."

Phoenix took a moment to think it over, then grunted. He was not completely sold on the plan, but when all was said and done, no one else had an alternative. Morgan and

Alvin did not offer any objections themselves. With that in mind, the plan was settled on.

They spent the rest of the afternoon preparing. They moved the bed aside so that when it was time, they would be able to teleport. Simon and Morgan came up with good excuses to tell anyone who may suspect them of wrongdoing. Phoenix practiced the messaging spell, so the group knew what to expect. Alvin tried to see the future to determine if they would be successful, but alas, the spell failed. Finally, Simon thought of ways to convince Cassandra to destroy Virgil.

When it was getting late, and curfew was likely to be set in motion, they met one last time to finalize the details. For once, Alvin cast a spell successfully, and saw that Archmage's office was empty. That was all they needed to carry on. Simon was confident that the plan would come together.

"This is going to work," Simon declared in a group huddle.

"I hope you're right," Phoenix said quietly. "If not, we're all expelled."

"And if we're all expelled, we should find a way to meet up," Simon said with a smile. "And I mean it. Once I'm done here, I'm going back to the normal life."

"Simon, you're giving up this life?" Morgan asked, worried.

"It's a very long story that I'm sure I'll share one day," Simon sighed. "I live in Santiago's Shield, California. I know I told you all this before, but I just wanted to remind you. I'm thinking I'll put my magic to good work. Not like what I'm doing with stage magic. Something worthwhile."

"Doesn't sound too bad," Alvin noted softly. "I wouldn't mind something like that. I'll look you up if I'm ever in the area."

"It… it isn't a dream I would want," Phoenix admitted. "I have a legacy to live up to. But I won't blame you for your dream. I will try my best to keep in touch with you when all is said and done."

"I understand, Phoenix," Simon turned to Morgan, hearing her sob, "Morgan, we'll still find a way to stay in touch. And I mean it, not like what I told all of my old high school friends."

Morgan laughed at the joke. "I know that. I'm just going to miss you all when this is all over. I'm… it's nothing. Let's get this over with."

The four pulled each other into a group hug. Simon cried a single tear before reminding himself that he needed to be strong. This was what he was going to miss the most about the world of magicians. Not the magic, but rather, the friends he made along the way. He had hoped to stay in contact with them after all this time but was unsure if that would be true.

"This is just the start of our journey," Simon declared. "Let's see that Virgil is destroyed. For good this time."

The group parted from the hug. Alvin sat down on his bed and waved his friends off when they left his room. Simon led the way down the hallway, flanked by Phoenix and Morgan. He felt confident in his plan. This would put an end to Darius' schemes once and for all.

Or, that's what he hoped.

Simon thought back to Alvin's cryptic sleep predictions. Could this be the start of the final battle? Or was it even a prophecy at all? Prophecies are supposed to rhyme, was what Simon thought with some doubt in his mind. Still, he was confident that if this was the final battle, they were about to come out as the victors. This was their story.

.

Before we get into how the heist went, let's take a moment to talk about friendship. I'll admit that the last part is a little bit cheesy (and relies too much on the "magic of friendship" junk) but one thing I brought up is a serious problem facing the youth of today.

Something I have learned through experience is that making friends is easy. Back when I was in public school, I was able to befriend just about anyone I set my mind out too. Making friends is about having the courage to walk up to a stranger and to say hi. That's all there is to it. Making friends is easy.

Keeping friends is hard.

You can make dozens of friends while you're in school or attending some sort of camp. You might start a group chat so you can stay in touch after everyone goes their separate ways. But in the end, people will forget to message back. After all is done, you're probably going to have a handful of friends at most to stay in touch with.

That's what happened to me. When I dropped out, I tried to stay in touch with all my old friends. But eventually, those friendships fade away, and we all move on. I didn't even have that handful of friends to fall back on.

I made it very clear that I have made a lot of mistakes, and that you shouldn't make my mistakes. So, do better. Have that handful of friends become two handfuls of friends. Arrange for group reunions whenever everyone's in town.

Just do whatever it takes to keep those friends. You're going to miss them, just you watch.

Thankfully, I was also learning from my own mistakes. I planned on doing whatever it took to stay in touch with my small group of friends (not like I knew any other students during my time at the Academy). And I had a feeling that they would stay in touch with me, too.

Alright. I'll admit that foiling a necromancer's plans does form a certain bond that you won't find anywhere else. But don't let that stop you from keeping friends.

Now, where was I? The heist of Virgil the Damned!

In hindsight, that was a terrible plan. Yep, still learning from my mistakes.

"Simon, how could your master plan have possibly failed?!" you say. Well, let me start off by making the hardest confession known to mankind.

I was wrong.

It all started when I remembered something important…

Chapter 17

"I forgot my cane."

Phoenix and Morgan both walked past Simon before looking back at him.

"I need to go get it," Simon turned around to walk back.

"Are you serious?" Simon heard Phoenix said as he facepalmed. "You can walk just fine."

"Sure, but that cane is part of my style, and also my signature weapon," Simon smirked. "I'll be right back. You two go on without me."

"Couldn't you just teleport to your room?" Morgan pointed out.

"Already halfway there!" Simon called back.

Simon jogged back to his room. Honestly, he felt that if everything was going this smoothly, he wouldn't need his cane to fight with. At this point, it only made sense that he had it by his side. It, the hat, the trench coat, it was all coming together to form his style.

Simon arrived at his dorm door and opened it. "Hey Alvin. Sorry, but I forg-"

Simon interrupted himself with a gasp. Alvin collapsed on the ground, groaning in pain. Darius Murdoch stepped out of the teleportation circle with a grin clear on his face.

"Simon, how good it is to see you," Darius greeted. "I must thank you for providing the way to my ancestor."

Without hesitation, Simon slammed the door shut and dashed towards Archmage's office.

"Morgan! Phoenix!" Simon yelled out when his friends came into sight. "Trouble!"

"Calm down, Simon!" Phoenix ordered when he finally caught up. "You're going to raise the alarm."

"That is the least of our worries right now," Simon breathed deeply while trying to capture his breath. "Darius is here."

"He is?" Morgan asked.

"He is, and he took down Alvin and-"

"-is on his way to retrieve his ancestor."

Simon saw the shocked look on Phoenix and Morgan's face and looked over his shoulder. Darius certainly was taking his time with his advance indicated by his leisurely pace. Two blue fireballs formed at his hand, although he made no attempt to attack the trio. Of course, why would he bother with an attack? They were outclassed. This was their warning: get in his way and fall. If only they had a professor.

Phoenix stepped in front of Simon, forming his own fireball in his hands.

"Get Virgil and get out of here. I will buy you as much time as I can."

"Phoenix, you're going to get hurt," Simon told him. "Run with us."

"Phoenix?" Darius paused in his walk and looked at Phoenix closely. "I thought you looked familiar. You look exactly like your father. A shame what happened to him, just like your mother. I didn't want to kill them, but they wouldn't settle for anything other than a fight to the death."

"Grah!" Phoenix roared out and threw his fireball at Darius.

"Come on, Simon!" Morgan grabbed his wrist, and they both ran.

It pained Simon to leave behind another friend to face unstoppable odds. Phoenix was the most proficient of the group in combat. Yet, he couldn't hold a flame compared to Darius' power. Simon cursed and tried not to think too much about Phoenix. Darius didn't kill Alvin. He wouldn't kill Phoenix. He would likely beat him to an inch of his life and leave him alive, but he wouldn't kill a child. Would he?

Simon and Morgan arrived at Archmage's office. The door was locked, of course, but the glass window on the door certainly wasn't. Simon broke the window down with a smash of his forearm, thankful for his thick coat, and opened the door. He immediately walked to the bookcase and pulled the lever to open it. The jar that held Virgil's soul awaited them at the end of the chamber.

"Virgil, we're leaving!" Simon said out loud.

How wonderful. That must mean my descendant is finally here.

"He won't get here fast enough!" Simon declared.

"I beg to differ!" Darius said, standing in the door frame

Simon turned towards the open door only for blue fire to knock him down onto his back. He grimaced and worked on unbuttoning his coat. The flames were spreading over it but had yet to burn his skin. He quickly tossed his coat off right as he saw Darius grab Morgan and pull her into the chamber.

Time slowed down for Simon as he tried to think of how to turn this situation around. Darius was advancing on Virgil's jar, and with Morgan as his shield, he dared not try to intercept him. He knew no spells to hurt or harm his advance. The battle was over when Darius arrived.

Simon could not hope to stop Darius.

The only one who possibly had a chance was Archmage.

Simon grinned. He reached over to Archmage's desk. "Darius, you still have one last opponent to face!"

"You're not even worth the spell, my boy," Darius called back, not even stopping.

"I know I am not, but I know who is," Simon brought the microphone of the intercom to his mouth and pressed the button. "Archmage."

A second later, Archmage appeared in front of Simon. "Good evening, Darius."

"No!" Darius exclaimed and reached for Virgil's phylactery. "You're too late!"

"I can make time for you."

Before Simon realized, the situation changed. Morgan was still in the chamber, but she was off to the side between the Orb of Foresight and the Fang of Arachne, safely out of Darius' reach. As for Darius, although he had reached for the jar that held Virgil, an invisible wall blocked his hand. The master of necromancy let out a scream of rage, then turned back to face Archmage.

"How?!" Darius shouted.

"I stopped time," Archmage said as if it was nothing.

"He stopped time!" Simon acted as a hype man to Archmage.

"I secured your hostage and erected a barrier over Virgil's phylactery," Archmage explained. "As long as I remain concentrated on maintaining that barrier, you will not get it."

"You're done now, Darius!"

Darius slowly grinned. "No. Stopping time is your most powerful spell, and that barrier will distract you from battle. Meanwhile, I am at my full strength. You should have killed me when you had the chance to."

"The safety of my students is my utmost priority," Archmage stepped into the chamber, followed by Simon. "They are the future."

Simon stopped suddenly. What Archmage said reminded Simon of something that would spell their doom. The master falls victim protecting his future during the battle. Darius was not the master. He was weak compared to Archmage, the true master. And as an educator, a headmaster of his own academy, the students were his future.

"Let's see you maintain two barriers then," Darius declared. "Face my most powerful spell!"

Darius extended his hand out to Simon and unleashed a mighty wave of blue flames. The flames tore apart the relics and knocked them down across the floor.

Archmage stepped in front of Simon, projecting a barrier to hold out against the attack.

Simon was now convinced that Archmage was going to die. Not only were the students his future, but he also admitted that he wanted Simon to succeed him. He was to be the future Archmage. Now, Archmage was holding out against Darius' most powerful attack. The veteran magician was struggling to hold out against the spell, his knees buckling.

Simon killed the most powerful magician on this planet with his stupid plan.

While casting his spell, Darius reached back for Virgil's phylactery. The barrier remained to block his way. This surprised both the necromancer and Simon. Slowly, Archmage walked forward, holding his protective shield. Slowly, the flames died away, and Archmage stood up straighter, stronger than before, and Virgil was still out of reach.

"I am definitely missing something here," Simon whispered.

"It's over, Darius," Archmage declared. "Your most powerful spell was nothing."

On the contrary, I'd say it made for quite the distraction.

Archmage let out a gasp as Morgan stabbed a dagger into his side.

"I'm sorry," she whispered

Simon was speechless as Archmage fell down to the ground, dagger between his ribs. His first reaction was to run up to the headmaster and check on him. He was still breathing, thankfully, but he grimaced in pain. Simon then looked up to Morgan, who took a few steps away from her victim. He was still trying to wrap his mind around her sudden betrayal.

Are you proud, Darius? I certainly am.

"As proud as any father could be," Darius nodded in agreement. "Morgan, I believe you've earned the honor of collecting our ancestor. I'm going to clean up the mess."

"Yes, father," Morgan walked over to Darius and Virgil.

"Seriously," Simon glared towards Morgan. "After all we've been through, you'll stand as a lackey to a villain?"

Morgan offered no defense, but Darius stepped in.

"I knew that Archmage needed to find a new and young recruit to replace him, someone outside of the system," Darius started. "I saw to it that Morgan learned not only necromancy, but displacement, support magic, and most important of all, enchantment When I sent her here, it was so she could charm this replacement, and in doing so, find a way to Virgil's phylactery. It worked perfectly. Sure, I had to let you escape with your brother at one point, but that failure was worth it."

Simon glared at Morgan. She picked up Virgil's phylactery and looked away from Simon. It was all starting to make sense. She had been in communication with her father all this time. She befriended him, made him fall for her, all so she could reveal his secrets. She knew about the displacement circle in his room, granting Darius entrance to the school. She had the training to teleport to Santiago's Shield and the ability to block out Archmage's divinations.

She had been his number one supporter since day one, pushing him ever closer to Virgil.

"Come on," Simon gestured to Archmage. "A dagger is a real mundane way to die for a magician. Get up."

"I… can't. I'm a dead man walking already," Archmage wheezed.

"Don't be overdramatic," Simon turned towards Archmage.

Simon's hopes were destroyed when he saw that it was the Fang of Arachne currently embedded into his side.

"How poetic that you say that, Archmage," Darius held out his hand. "I think I will raise you as my newest servant to show the true power of-"

"DARIUS!" Professor Brenton's voice boomed out through the hall.

"And it looks like I have to speed this up," Darius conjured a blue flame. "Any last words."

"I'm not done yet," Archmage declared, and through gritted teeth, pulled himself back on his feet. "I can stall long enough for Solomon to get here. Unlike me, he will show no mercy to you."

Darius paused, and took a moment to think. "We're leaving, Morgan."

Before Simon could react, the father and daughter teleported away. Simon stood up, standing by Archmage's side. What seemed like it would be a perfect victory had turned into a horrible defeat. No, worse than that. The end of the world. He did not want to think about Morgan's betrayal or Archmage's injury. His thoughts turned elsewhere.

"Archmage," Simon whispered.

"Yes, Mr. Crowley?"

"Why did you tell him that?" Simon asked. "If you didn't, we could have stopped him with Professor Brenton."

"Ah, but I wanted him to run," Archmage smirked. "What I said was a bluff. He could have killed me here and be done with it."

Archmage let out one final chuckle before he collapsed onto Simon, who caught him. And with nothing else to occupy his attention, only one thought came to mind.

"I was wrong," Simon thought out loud.

.

Important lesson: if you plan to steal something that you are supposed to protect, you are just asking for something to go wrong. And it took a strong case of hindsight for me to see that now.

So, a lot happened then. Let me just give a brief summary of what happened to show you all how badly things turned out to be because of me.

Darius had the phylactery of Virgil the Damned.

Morgan was the mole all along and got away with Darius.

Archmage was dying.

Even today, I struggle to wrap my mind around the layers of the plan that relied solely on my disregard of the academy and the advice of Archmage. That just really shows how predictable I was, and I hate that.

I also try not to think too much about how Morgan used me either. I never saw it coming, not like that at least. It just made me realize that everything from our first meeting was just her following through with her father's plans. She played me, and I couldn't see it until after the damage was done.

Either I'm too paranoid or I'm too trusting. There is no in between for me.

I wasn't mad at her though. I wasn't mad at Darius or Virgil. I was mad at myself for being such an idiot. I still have these occasional thoughts that have me questioning if what I am doing is the right choice to make or if I am walking right into what my enemy wants me to do.

My regrets haunt me whenever I think about them. I put on a facade as THE STYLISH SIMON! and I like putting on that act. It takes my mind off of the problems with the world. For the most part, I am the act.

The reason I bring this up now is because after that horrible defeat, the act I put on wasn't going to save me. My mind wrapped itself around all of my doubts and all of my failures.

When Professor Brenton arrived at the office, he put a lot of the blame on me. I did not resist as he sent me away to be locked up in his classroom, for my own safety and the safety of the academy. Archmage was taken to the medical ward to recover on his own.

Chapter 18

The combative classroom was somewhere Simon had never been to before, and after the night was over, he doubted he would ever return. There was no way anyone would want him to be a student at the academy anymore.

There were no desks in the combative classroom. There were only benches that circle around a large ring, indicated by the lines drawn on the ground. There were training dummies, new and scorched alike, scattered across the room. Simon recalled Phoenix mentioning that combative class was about practical practice with very little on battle theory. Based off of his descriptions, Simon thought he would have had fun blasting training dummies with fire and not worrying about written tests.

Simon hoped that Phoenix was alright. Alvin too. He hadn't heard from either of them since the failure of their heist.

Simon rested on one of the benches and covered his face with his top hat with his cane resting on his lap. This was his defeat. Darius was preparing the ritual to bring Virgil the Damned back to his old form, and then, Santiago's Shield would be swarmed with undead monsters. Not like there was anything he could do to stop it. If he involved himself anymore, then he was likely to make things worse.

Professor Brenton, or rather, Interim Headmaster Brenton, could handle it.

Goosebumps formed on Simon. The classroom was definitely becoming colder.

It was not freezing cold but there was a change in temperature. Simon grabbed his hat and sat up on the bench to put it back on. Aside from the cold, the room was also growing darker. Then, a bright white light formed in the center of the dueling circle. It materialized into a door, and now, Simon was on his feet. This was not normal.

The door opened, and from it, a spectral image of Archmage floated out from it.

"Mr. Crowley," Archmage greeted.

"Archmage!" Simon gasped. "You're a ghost!"

"Don't be ridiculous," Archmage chuckled. "I am simply reaching out to you with my consciousness through the use of my magic. I am still alive."

"And that's any less ridiculous?"

"It is what it is. Mr. Crowley, why are you sitting and moping around about your failures?"

"My failure led to your death. Or is leading to your death. Is there a way you can project your consciousness that isn't all spectral like?"

"You were not the one that stabbed me," Archmage pointed out.

"No, but I led the one who did to the dagger," Simon argued. "I trusted her, so I brought danger upon you."

"And you trusted Alvin and Phoenix," Archmage countered. "They are both waiting for the chance to take the fight to Darius."

"Then they can fight with Professor Brenton."

"Professor Brenton is one who reacts," Archmage explained. "He does not know where Darius is--"

"The Santiago Mausoleum in Santiago's Shield, California," Simon interrupted.

"--and until he has solid evidence on where Darius is, he will wait before he acts rather than expend resources chasing a possible dead end."

"And none of my friends can get to Santiago's Shield," Simon realized.

"Correct. Phoenix's emotions rule over him while Alvin is afraid. They not only need you to get there, but they need you to come up with a plan."

"I can't," Simon sighed. "The last plan I came up with ended up with Darius beating all of my friends."

"Simon, I cannot defeat Darius. You can. Right now, Darius is as vulnerable as he will ever be. It will be a long fight, but if anyone can come up with a plan to overcome him, it will be you."

Simon thought it over. It was going to take a miracle for three magicians in training, two of which without offensive magic, to win. Darius may be expending all of his magic right now, but he certainly wasn't defenseless. Morgan, his student, knew more than enchantments. Then, there was Eustace, who held no magic, but certainly could stab someone with that dagger of his.

Also, the Santiago Mausoleum was a graveyard. There was likely already an army of undead corpses waiting for them.

Yet, what if there was a way for Darius to be defeated? Simon had an idea of how to do so, but that would mean getting past the defenses. If he could do that and slip in to confront Darius, then perhaps the battle could turn in their favor. A plan formulated in his mind. It might not be the best plan, but at the very least, he had one.

That was not the only realization Simon came to.

"Thanks, Archmage," Simon smiled. "Thanks for snapping me back to my senses, and for jumping in front of that dagger for me."

"You are welcome, Mr. Crowley."

"And you're not Archmage," Simon declared. "Did you really have to go over the top with the illusions, Cassandra?"

The image of Archmage grew silent, then spoke in a feminine voice. "Was it really that obvious."

"You called me by my first name and already demonstrated you can make an Archmage illusion," Simon pointed out. "Still, thank you. I'll stop your brother for you."

"And I thank you for that," Cassandra's voice was somber. "Darius is evil, but my family situation is very complicated. Take care, Simon."

The illusion of Archmage disappeared, the temperature returned to normal, and the darkness faded away. Simon still had much to learn about the art of illusions, but with what he already knew, it may be enough to stop Darius. It had to be.

Simon focused, concentrating on the teleportation circle. It was time to leave detention early.

When he popped into his own room, he was met with a heavy tome slamming into his shoulder.

"Grah!" Simon gasped in pain and fell down.

"Oh," Alvin, sitting on his bed, looked in confusion. "Sorry. I was afraid you were Darius again."

"No, I deserved that," Simon stood up and dusted himself off. "Why didn't you just clear off the teleportation circle?"

Alvin paused to think. "You know, that's a good idea."

"Never mind! Where's Phoenix?" Simon grabbed his cane.

"In his room. I think Darius was holding back. He didn't want to harm his future students permanently."

"Well, that's his first mistake. I'm getting Phoenix so we can stop Darius."

"Yeah, about that," Alvin looked up to the ceiling. "I've been thinking, and well, I'm probably just going to hold you back, so…"

"You're scared, aren't you?" Simon interrupted.

Alvin remained silent, then nodded. "I thought I was going to die."

"I get it. I'm scared too. This is a life or death scenario, and all of the adults are letting teenagers go against some of the most powerful necromancers out there. But if we don't do anything, he wins anyways. This is the only way."

"I'm not like you or Phoenix," Alvin sighed in defeat. "I'm not a fighter. I can barely work any magic myself."

"Yet you were able to figure out what was happening in your sleep," Simon encouraged with a friendly grin. "If you want to walk away now, you can. I won't stop you. But I can promise you that if you come, you can help, even without your magic."

Alvin paused again and took a deep breath. "I'm in. But if I die, I'm blaming you."

"We're not going to die," Simon promised. "Let's go."

The two left the room together. Simon was hesitant about bringing Alvin into danger. Just like he admitted, he wasn't much of a fighter, and he was scared of their foes. However, Alvin was someone good in heart, and someone Simon needed with him on the battlefield. Simon was going to need all the help he could get, and he was already thinking of ways to bring in more help. One knock on the neighboring door later, and Phoenix answered.

"Simon!" Phoenix greeted, shocked to see his friend.

"We don't have time," Simon told him. "I'm going out to stop Darius. You in or not?"

"I'm in," Phoenix grinned. "I have to fight."

"And you'll get the chance to fight."

"Is there any way we can get to Darius now?" Alvin asked.

"Not quite," Simon admitted. "I could try teleporting us to the Mausoleum, but that's too risky. The teleportation circle back at my house is still active, so we can go there, then head to the Mausoleum from there."

"Let's not waste any time then," Phoenix declared. "Every second we waste is another second for Virgil to return."

Simon grabbed Alvin and Phoenix by the hands, ready to teleport them to his home. Together, the three of them would be able to handle Morgan and Darius. Eustace and the undead army will be another problem, but Simon wasn't done with calling in reinforcements yet. With a nod from his friends, Simon teleports the group back into his attic.

"Alright, I need you to be quiet," Simon whispered. "My family is sleeping at this hour. Head outside. I'll meet you there."

Phoenix and Alvin nodded. Slowly, they lowered the ladder that led down to the hallway, and climbed down. Simon directed his friends out to the front door, then made his way to his own bedroom. Scott and Seth were asleep right now. Simon was careful to tiptoe over to Scott so not to wake up Seth, then shook his brother lightly.

"Scottie," Simon whispered. "It's me, Scottie. I need your help."

"Simon?" Scott yawned and woke up. "What are you doing back so soon?"

"I may have dropped the ball and Virgil the Damned may be close to coming back," Simon told him.

"You did what?!" Scott whispered harshly. Simon was thankful Seth was a heavy sleeper.

"Our family will be safe thanks to Professor Montague. I'm going to make things better, but I need your help."

"Simon, I'm not a magician. I want to help, but what are you expecting me to do?"

"Bash some zombie's heads in like in those video games you like to play," Simon grinned.

Scott took a moment to think. "How many are we talking about?"

"A whole graveyard of them?"

"And you expect me to emerge out of this fight alive?" Scott asked in disbelief.

"Well, you're not going to be doing it alone," Simon assured him. "Do you think Zack is awake right now?"

"He's throwing a party," Scott yawned. "I just got back from it."

"Good. Tell him that he needs to move his party to Santiago's Mausoleum. And tell him to bring as many blunt instruments as he can."

"Do you really think I can convince him?"

"Maybe. If anyone can, it's you. You're my brother, after all," Simon told him. "And if you don't, well, I'm probably going to die, and then Santiago's Shield is going to fall to a zombie apocalypse."

"Woah," Scott muttered.

"Just reminding you of the odds," Simon said. "If you can't convince Zack, come back and protect the others for me."

Simon quickly hugged his brother then stood up. It pained him to drag family into this, but without some form of reinforcements, the plan was not going to work. Simon relied solely on the calvary to give him the distraction to slip past Darius' defenses and confront him. If all of the pieces came together, then they would emerge as the victors of the upcoming conflict.

Before leaving his house, Simon grabbed a baseball bat and held it alongside his cane. Phoenix and Alvin were waiting outside on the sidewalk. Simon handed Alvin the bat, then ran towards Santiago's Mausoleum. Phoenix and Alvin followed after him, and as they ran, Simon started to think of how exactly he could defeat someone as powerful as Darius, a very daunting task.

Now, this was definitely something I would not have seen coming before learning about magic: building a plan and giving Zack an important role. You're wondering how I could forgive someone who has tormented me for so long, and that answer is simpler than you may realize.

Compared to all of the necromancers that had plans of changing the status quo of both the regular and magical world, Zack's thuggish ways were not really too much of a concern for me.

I might be a little too trusting at times, but if my forgiveness gets Zack to help, that's an advantage. Also, he doesn't seem to bully Scott too much, which is a plus.

Bringing Scott down to the battlefield was more on my mind then. I was worried about him getting hurt. I was afraid that I could lose him, just like I was when he was with Darius.

Yet, as an older brother, I need to learn to accept that all of my little brothers and sisters are going to grow up. Scott definitely was old enough to start making his own choices. Not an adult just yet but old enough to have the freedom to decide who he hangs out with or if he wanted to throw down with the undead.

Also, Darius did kidnap him, so there was some retribution to be given out.

And I just realized how poetic that sounds. Two Crowley brothers coming together to fight against the

Murdochs, the family that had caused them so much pain. Talk about a comeback story.

So, if Zack came through in the end (I wish I had more backup than my old bully), that would mean Eustace and any undead minions would be dealt with. If they didn't come through, Phoenix, Alvin, and I were probably dead.

We already had our work cut out for us even with Zack's help. We had the "honor" of fighting two powerful magicians.

Morgan would be the first to oppose us. That didn't surprise me at all. She stood guard over the graveyard, to ensure that the ritual wasn't interrupted.

I wish that she only knew necromancy and enchantments, but I didn't want to lie to myself. She had to have drawn that teleportation circle in the basement. If she knew displacement, what's to stop her from knowing all of the other schools of magic?

Absolutely nothing.

I wasn't going to fight her. Not after she nearly killed me during my first visit to the graveyard.

Phoenix would fight her.

Chapter 19

"We need to press on," Phoenix said, determined. "The longer we wait, the more of a fight we'll be in for."

"We wait for the calvary," Simon insisted. "We go in guns blazing, we won't be able to stop Darius."

Phoenix glared in the direction of the graveyard. The trio stood on a sidewalk outside of the Santiago Mausoleum. Even in the darkness, they could make out shambling figures, moving about. After several minutes of observation, Simon could tell that they were growing in numbers. Someone was actively raising corpses to defend the graveyard.

Simon hoped that it was Darius raising the corpses. Or perhaps Eustace finally learned the secrets of magic. Unfortunately, he knew better. Morgan was out there, willingly defiling the dead to aid her father in his mad scheme.

This was not something Simon was looking forward to. It hadn't even been a day since she stabbed him in the back, and already, they were about to have their second confrontation. Simon struggled to find the confidence to fight Morgan as an enemy. She was a good double agent. There would be no redemption, especially after what she did to

Archmage, but he could not stop himself from hoping that she would help.

Thankfully, he had Phoenix and Alvin behind him. He was going to have to work with Alvin in dealing with the undead. Phoenix would serve as Morgan's opponent, and unlike Simon, he would not hold back. She was the daughter of the man who killed his parents. It was only fitting that they would fight.

And unfortunately, that only made him impatient.

"How do you know Zack and his gang have enough people to contend with Morgan's army?" Phoenix asked.

"He has about two dozen people to attend parties," Simon explained, "and thankfully, Morgan isn't creating anything like the abomination that almost killed us in the basement. They can handle themselves."

"And so can we."

"Phoenix, I get that you're frustrated with waiting, but think about it," Simon started. "In our way, we have an army of zombies. Then, there's Morgan. And somewhere in there is Eustace. And finally, we have Darius."

"And you think two dozen people are going to stand a chance?" Alvin said in between practice swings of his bat.

"Do we have any other choice?" Simon asked.

A noise unlike any other interrupted their conversation--a tormented, ear-splitting screech. Back at the graveyard, a translucent stream of blue essence was flowing out of the various tombstones. The color matched those of the necromancy spells Simon had witnessed. And then, he realized that the essence was not just any essence. They were the souls of the deceased in the graveyard.

The spirits flew towards the sky, where black clouds started to form over the mausoleum itself. They began to funnel down towards the roof of the structure, breaking through. Simon gulped and clutched his cane even tighter. Virgil the Damned was coming back. He was coming back stronger than ever. And they were running out of time to stop the ritual before it was too late.

"So, are we going to stand around to watch the view?" Phoenix scoffed and stormed forward to the graveyard.

"Right, right," Simon followed after him. "So, the calvary is going to be a little late, but we can manage."

"Sure we can," Alvin sighed and gripped his bat tightly with both hands.

"We will have to. I will get Morgan's attention, and as much of the undead, on me. You two can slip in and stop Darius. Somehow. Do you have a plan?"

"I'm still working out the details and *wait a minute*," Simon quickly picked up the pace. "No way I am letting you do a heroic sacrifice."

"If I die, then let it be stopping Darius."

"I am not letting you die," Simon declared. "We'll hold the zombies off until the cavalry arrives."

"Fighting zombies does sound more fun than facing Darius," Alvin shuddered.

"And if Zack doesn't come?"

"Then it was nice to fight by your side one last time," Simon smiled. "To the both of you."

The three walked side-by-side and stepped into the graveyard. The undead, consisting of both skeletons and decomposing bodies, made no attempt to stop them. Simon slowly smiled. If this meant what he thought it meant, then that changed everything. If Morgan was ready to try to make up for what she did, then Virgil the Damned was as good as dead.

Yet, after seeing her, Simon had his doubts. Morgan stood on the path that led towards the mausoleum. She wore the black robes she previously had on during the attack, as well as half of her shattered mask. If that was not a good sign, then neither was the cruel half-smile she had on.

"Morgan!" Simon called out. "We don't have to do this."

"Such a hypocrite," Morgan shot back. "You would do anything for your family. When I do something for mine, I'm suddenly the villain?

Simon remained silent, both from her sudden and unexpected cruelty and that she had a point. "Then why did you let us come this far without attacking? That's because you want us to win."

"It's because I lured you into a trap," Morgan cackled. "You're surrounded by my undead warriors now."

"You know, I thought that after you betrayed me, I couldn't feel any dumber. I was wrong."

"Enough!" Phoenix shouted, throwing two bolts of fire towards Morgan. "Stop listening to her! We must fight!"

Morgan raised a faint shield to block the fire bolts. With a wave of her hand, dozens of risen corpses started to advance on the two. They moved a slight pace, not too fast, but still threatening. Phoenix ignored the advancing foes, conjuring more spells of flame, lightning, and ice to blast at Morgan. That left Simon and Alvin to fend off the army for as long as he could.

Simon had to rely on his short-range teleportation to keep Phoenix safe. He teleported to the nearest skeleton, and with a swing of his cane, sent its bones crashing down. Unfortunately, there was no time to rest, and he had to lean away from a corpse's wild swing. None of the undead were armed with weapons but Simon was confident they probably had some weird zombie curse on them. Better to be in one piece as a human rather than a walking corpse.

Simon continued to teleport across the battlefield, wielding his cane as a weapon to bash down any corpses nearing Phoenix. Alvin kept to Phoenix's side, taking down any undead that Simon missed while avoiding spells from Morgan. It was tough and tiring work to keep up the pace throughout the battle. Minutes flew by with the two magicians trying to keep their friend safe. Simon was thankful for the physical training he underwent during recovery. He continued his workout since then, allowing him to keep up. The old Simon would have fallen over, exhausted, long ago.

Meanwhile, Phoenix and Morgan both exchanged flames, blue and orange alike. Their support spells held, and neither were damaged. However, Simon quickly realized that between them, Phoenix was the more experienced battler. He threw a lightning bolt, which Morgan blocked with ease, with one hand, while spinning the other hand. The gesture confused Simon until he saw Morgan slowly being lifted up in the air, a cyclone forming around her.

"Your necromancy spells cannot compare to the might of combative magic!" Phoenix declared.

Morgan was around fifteen feet in the air when the cyclone sent her flying down to the dirt. She groaned in pain, and the undead stopped advancing. Without a commander, they just stood uselessly. The three magicians both took this moment to breathe. The battle was taking a little effort from their part, so the break was necessary.

"Things are going too easy," Alvin

"She's done for," Phoenix walked towards the mausoleum. "I think we might be able to take down Darius no problem."

Simon nods in agreement. "Eustace won't be too much of a problem if the zombies are passive. That leaves Darius. And between the three of us, we stand a chance."

"Simon…" Morgan called out weakly. "I'm sorry."

Simon stopped in his tracks. That sounded like the old Morgan. Slowly, he turned around, walking to where she was, broken on the ground. She had her head lifted up, showing a somber expression on half of her face. Her hand was lifted towards Simon. He took a step toward her, with Alvin and Phoenix watching.

"Simon don't get close to her," Phoenix warned. "The last time you did, she stabbed Archmage."

"I was just doing what my father wanted," Morgan muttered.

"She's just someone trying to do what her father told her," Simon continued to walk toward her. "I think that fighting us might have helped her."

"She stabbed Archmage," Phoenix recalled.

"I was there, Phoenix," Simon noted.

"And what about those insults she traded with us just now?"

"That wasn't me," Morgan coughed.

"It wasn't her."

"Damn it, Simon," Phoenix cursed and stormed after him. "Can't you see-"

"Leave us alone," Morgan motioned her hand towards Phoenix and Alvin. "The both of you."

Phoenix stopped in his tracks and fell silent. Alvin looked at him, then back at Simon, confused on what was happening.

Simon moved closer to Morgan, compelled to do so to help her. He knelt by her. She looked very weak to him, in need of help. She reached out a single hand towards him and closed her eyes. Simon gently took her hand into his and smiled. He forgot about her betrayal, only interested in forgiving and helping her.

Suddenly, Morgan gasped. "You need to run."

"Huh?"

Morgan closed her eyes, grinned, and started to drain Simon's life from him.

Simon screamed in pain when Morgan tightened her grip on him and started to drain him of his life once more. It was as painful as the first time she used that spell on him during the first trip to the graveyard. The drain had left him defeated and on the mend for a week.

This was how he would lose to the Murdochs.

Simon heard Alvin shout but could not decipher his words. Morgan grabbed his face with both hands to drain his life. He tried to break out but his strength grew weaker with each moment. Morgan locked eyes with him as she continued to slowly kill him and laugh. He fell victim to her enchantment, and so did Phoenix.

Fortunately, Alvin's mind remained his own.

Alvin slammed his bat into Morgan, shattering the other half of her mask and knocking her away from Simon. They both fell onto the ground, with Alvin trying to attack Morgan while she was on the ground. Simon fumbled around for the ground and sighed in relief to find his cane. He slowly lifted himself up onto his knees while Alvin kept missing with his bat. Morgan, completely energized, was able to roll away from him and got back on her feet. Blue fires completely climbed up her arm and the undead seemed more aggravated than before.

Alvin, seeing the murderous look Morgan gave her, took several steps back. She flung a blue fireball at him, and out of poor instinct, Alvin raised his bat to cover him like a shield. Simon was able to save him with a quick tackle. However, it left them both exposed on the ground. Phoenix was able to get to the two in time to block the second blue fire attack. Yet, his incorporeal shield, conjured in such short notice, shattered, and his flame was set aflame. Alvin stood back up as Phoenix beat his hand against his coat rapidly to put the fires out.

"She's back at full strength!" Phoenix exclaimed in pain. "I'm sorry."

"Don't apologize," Alvin said and picked up his bat. "She enchanted us, or at least, tried to with me."

"It takes a feeble mind to resist my mind enchantments," Morgan laughed as the undead closed in.

"Something felt off about what just happened," Simon raised himself back onto a single knee.

"Worry about that later. Can you two keep the undead off me again?" Phoenix asked. "I might be able to defeat her again."

"Not really," Simon chuckled. "I'm struggling to stand now."

"I'll try, but if it's down to me, I can't promise anything," Alvin said, eyeing each of the undead.

"This is the end of your story," Morgan taunted. "This is how you all die."

"The only people who are dying tonight are the zombies you brought back to life," said a voice from behind Morgan.

Simon smirked. Zack and his gang approached Morgan from behind. Each was armed with a baseball bat, a crowbar, a chain or some kind of weapon. Zack himself cracked his knuckles, choosing to fight with his fists. Morgan looked confused at the new arrivals.

"What's this?" Morgan asked with a mix of sarcasm and shock.

"The calvary," Simon answered.

"Let's send the dead back to their graves!" Zack shouted.

The gang cheered and ran off to battle against the undead. The undead charged back under Morgan's command. She turned back to face the magicians with barely enough time to block one of Phoenix's lightning bolts. Phoenix prepared more bolts of lightning, ready to continue their duel. Alvin bashed an incoming zombie with his bat and joined Zack's gang in the battle.

As for Simon, he pushed himself back onto his feet with his cane. The battle surrounded him, and thankfully, no one was making him his target. It was time to confront Darius. Even though each muscle of his body ached, and he felt so weak, he could beat the mastermind behind this wall. Slowly, Simon limped towards the mausoleum. Tonight, Virgil the Damned would fall.

.

You know what sounds exciting? A giant battle between a teenage street gang and a pack of wild undead, highlighted with a battle between two magicians.

I wish I could have stuck around for the battle and fought alongside Phoenix, Alvin, and Zack. But given my state, I was just going to get myself killed. Let the fighters handle their action while I continued my plan.

If I'm going to be honest, I thought that I was going to die. At the time, I already felt that I was one of the corpses that Morgan raised. I thought that was going to be my fate. Very happy thoughts, I know.

Let me also say that I didn't have to die in my attempt to save the day. I could teleport. Professor Montague supposedly made my house much harder to breach with her support magic, so I knew I could go back to my family and be safe. And if Virgil could breach through that, well, I could teleport my whole family to the academy, cross off the teleportation circle, and we're safe again.

What I am trying to say is that I could have left at any point. I didn't have to die a pointless death.

But I still had to put a stop to Darius. I still had to save the day.

I made a lot of mistakes. Those mistakes left me nearly dead and harmed others. My mistakes endangered my family.

Yet, when all is said and done, someone always comes in to save me. Archmage, Cassandra, Phoenix, Alvin, Scott and even Zack now. I owed these people everything. This was more about redemption. This was about repaying all my favors.

No one would come to help me face Darius. That didn't matter. This was something I had to do alone.

Chapter 20

Simon climbed up the hill. Each step was an exhausting step, even with his cane for support. His bones felt weaker than ever before, his muscles ached in agony, and he grew more tired. He regretted falling victim to her mind control and strengthening her. Simon was not sure what there was about her change in her behavior, from calling out to help as his friend to being a cruel and vicious magician, but that was going to be a story for another time.

Simon's body was telling him that he was going to fail. He was not even sure if he could make it to the top of the hill. Still, he pressed on, enduring through the pain and exhaustion as best he could. Perhaps he should have swapped places with Phoenix. He could only muster the strength for one more teleport, but if timed correctly, he might have gotten the jump on Morgan. Phoenix could win in a match against her. He couldn't win against Darius.

A student magician would not win in a straight out fight against Darius.

Simon was not going to give Darius a fight. As much as it pained him to admit it, the theories on illusions were what would save him today.

Simon made it to the doors of the mausoleum and groaned. He groaned not out of the pain he experienced now, but rather, the pain he would experience trying to open that door. Simon hated that it was not Darius that would stop him. Instead, it was a blasted door that was going to put a stop. He thought about it for a moment. Illusions were not going to help him, and in all honesty, he did not want to waste his one teleport getting through the door.

Simon was getting ready to call for Phoenix to blast it down (such as back in the library) when it creaked open. Eustace stepped out, knife in hand.

"What is the meaning of this?!" Eustace growled. "Master Murdoch is already frustrated enough with Virgil. He does not need this!"

"Darius having a bad night?" Simon rolled his eyes. "I can relate."

Eustace started to advance on Simon, who took a step back. He was hoping that if it came down to battle, Simon would be able to sneak up on them. However, there was no sneak attack. Simon cursed. Out of all of his opposition, he was originally least worried about Eustace. That was before he could barely lift his cane above his hip to use as a weapon.

"Hey!" Scott ran up next to Simon. He carried a baseball bat in his hands. "Glad I found you two."

"Good to see you too, Scottie," Simon smiled weakly.

"And the infestation continues to grow," Eustace snarled. "Master Murdoch didn't want me to cut you up when

I abducted you. He said that you would make for a potential student. Now that we are on the battlefield, I can kill you, and show Master Murdoch why I deserve to be his student."

"Honestly, as bad as a man as Darius is, he at least knows that psychopaths shouldn't be magicians," Simon taunted. "Scottie, you got this under control?"

"He held a knife to my throat when I was unarmed and starved me for days. I have a full stomach and a baseball bat in my hands. Plus, I've been looking for a chance to get back at him. I can take him."

Eustace charged forward, brandishing his knife. Simon could already tell that he had no clue how to fight with it aside from stabbing someone. Granted, Scott was a teenage boy, but a bat had a longer reach than a dagger. He first swung the knife out of the man's hand. He proceeded to follow it with a swing to the knee to knock Eustace down. Scott positioned it so that the handle was facing his foe's face, then knocked him out with a quick jab.

Simon let out a low whistle after seeing that display. All this time, he had been worried about Scott involving himself with Zack and his gang. After today, he knew his little brother could look out for himself.

"Good work," Simon approached the door, which was slightly open. "Mind standing guard over here? I'd rather not have a zombie interrupt my battle."

"I guess so," Scott turned back to face the battle, keeping an eye out for potential intruders. His eyes focused on the battle between Morgan and Phoenix. "So, is that battle going to be just like the battle with your friend?"

"No way," Simon chuckled. "I know illusions, I know how to teleport, and I know how to hit people with my cane. That's how I'm going to stop Darius."

Simon stepped inside and Scott hesitantly pushed the door closed behind him. Once inside, he was careful to lift his cane up from the ground. He would have to rely on his own strength to get him through the rest of the way. The element of surprise was one element he had over Darius. He could not blow that by having his cane tapping on the stone ground.

Simon took a deep breath in and focused on his plan. He was only going to get one chance for it to work. If he messed up at any point, Darius would win. The stakes were high. If his act dropped at any point, if his illusions were not enough, then he was as good as dead. He pushed those doubts aside one last time and focused on weaving his illusions.

Tonight, Simon was about to put on the show of a lifetime.

The chamber where Simon met Darius the first time was filled with the light of the soul's essence. On top of Virgil the Damned's coffin was his phylactery, where the souls were channeled into. Darius observed the ritual with a frown. Simon could tell that something was off when he finally stepped in. Hopefully, that would only help with his illusions.

"Sir Darius Murdoch!" Simon greeted, spreading his arms out wide. "Eustace told me that you were feeling frustrated."

"You!" Darius snapped. "What did Archmage do to my ancestor?! He has grown silent since we have left the academy. He will not respond to my calls. He will not return to his body. I offer him ancient souls and he still does not speak!"

"I know not of what problems there are," Simon bowed. "After all, your daughter did kill Archmage. You certainly jumped the gun with that."

"Then you are of no use to me!"

Darius threw a ball of blue flame at the man that taunted him in his waning moment of triumph. It passed through the illusion and Simon faded away.

"Missed me!" Simon appeared to his right, grinning.

"What is the meaning of this?!" Darius gasped in shock. "That should have killed you!"

"It should have, had it been me," Darius turned to his left to see another Simon.

"But alas," another Simon stood where the destroyed illusion had been. "Illusions are my trade."

"What are you doing?" Darius stepped forward, conjuring another blue fire into his hands.

"My favorite trick," the three Simons spoke in unison. "A variation of it to be exact. The shell game, where the shell is put under a cup, the cups are swapped around, and you pick the cup you think the shell is under. The real Stylish Simon is here, but you only get one chance to pick which of us is him."

"Referring to yourself in the third person now," Darius rolled his eyes. "And I only get one chance to pick the real one?"

"You do."

"Don't you show me the real Simon first before you swap him around?" Darius pointed out.

"I did say it was a variation of the shell game," the three Simons grinned.

"In that case, allow me to add another variation to the game!"

Darius slammed the blue flame into the ground, sending it out as a shockwave. It went towards his sides and forward from him, but not behind. He was careful with his spell. Even if Virgil was now silent for whatever reasons, Darius still made sure to keep him safe and not direct the shockwave in his direction. The shockwave slammed into the three Simons at once, with not a single chance to react.

The three illusions faded away when the flames started to dance around them.

"A valiant attempt," Simon's voice echoed throughout the chamber. "However, no matter how many variations you put on it, the shell game always has one constant rule: the shell is never under the cup to begin with."

"And you tell me this, why?!" Darius exclaimed, his frustrations taking over.

"A true magician never reveals his secrets," Simon answered, appearing behind Darius. "However, you're not going to be around long enough to share my secrets."

Simon charged forward with a sudden shout. He brandished his cane and pushed his legs off to strike at Darius. This was the moment that determined who would win the day. Darius turned around, and with hatred clear in his eyes, unleashed a barrage of blue flames towards Simon before he could hope to strike him.

The battle was over now.

The barrage destroyed the illusion and slammed into the phylactery that had been covered by Simon's illusion.

"No," Darius muttered. "NO!"

The phylactery was instantly destroyed. It shattered into many tiny pieces. And with its destruction, the souls within were released from the ritual, flowing away towards the ceiling before they vanished. Virgil would remain silent forever. Darius ran up to the coffin that held his ancestor, holding back the tears.

"No, Virgil, I didn't mean to do this," Darius exclaimed. "I meant to bring you back! To show the world that necromancy was supreme!"

"If it makes you feel any better, he was going to disown you if you lost to me," Simon stood behind Darius, leaning on his cane. "At least now, you can still call him family."

"Would you please stop taunting me with your illusions!"

Thwack.

Darius fell down with a thud after Simon's cane slammed into the side of his head.

"If you insist."

Throughout the entire confrontation, Simon was invisible, and only revealed himself after he won. He sighed and sat down on Virgil's coffin. Not like he would have minded. That swing took a lot out of him. The battle had been won, and now, the chamber was dark. Simon was glad that for whatever reason, Virgil did not answer the call of Darius. That frustrated him to no end, allowing for him to take out his anger on the illusions.

Still, there was a thought that was on Simon's mind. Virgil was insistent on his return. Yet, he made no attempt to return to his body. Something was not adding up. He heard footsteps coming down. Scott, Phoenix, and Alvin turned around the corner to enter the chamber.

That's when the realization struck Simon, and he gasped.

"It's just us," Scott assured him. "No reason to be scared. We just saw the sky returned to normal."

"You did it," Phoenix clapped. "You actually stopped Darius Murdoch!"

"Where's Morgan?" Simon asked.

Phoenix looked away. "She escaped after the souls stopped coming. Zack's cleaning up the rest of her undead army."

"No," Simon whispered.

"Simon, I know that you were crushing hard on her, but she tried to kill you," Alvin reminded him.

"That's not it," Simon shook his head. "I'm not upset that Morgan escaped. I'm upset that Virgil escaped."

You're welcome.

Hey, I am allowed to say that. Sure, Morgan/Virgil managed to escape, but guess what? I still stopped an undead army from invading North California. I mean, I'm pretty sure the military could have taken on a bunch of skeletons and zombies, but still, you're welcome.

I suppose this is something you would call a bittersweet victory. The true mastermind escaped by possessing a dear friend of mine and was out on the loose. But I like to think of it like this: if you take bittersweet out, it's victory!

At least, that's what I keep telling myself whenever I think about that night.

But really, the battle could have gone a lot worse. Phoenix took a few hits but nothing as major as me. Scott managed to hold his own and get revenge on Eustace. No one from Zack's gang was dead either, so that was a plus. Darius was down for the count. Asides from Virgil escaping, we did win.

There was a brief celebration after Darius was defeated. Zack and his gang celebrated by destroying the undead that remained in place. Phoenix even took in on the fun. I was barely able to stay awake, so I just stayed with Scott, who tied up Darius and Eustace.

After the celebration, we got our stories straight. Eustace was responsible for the disturbance in the graveyard and Zack saw that he was turned into the proper authorities. I later found out that Eustace was convicted under multiple charges, kidnapping included. The world won't have to worry about him again with him locked away in prison.

Darius was another story. No offense to whoever cares but there was no way that a normal jail cell was going to hold him. So, Phoenix, Alvin, and I had to take him back with us to the North American Academy for Magicians. Professor Brenton would come up with a way to ensure that Darius was locked away.

I told Scott that I would be back as soon as I could. I didn't imagine that turning in Darius would take that long. Phoenix grabbed onto him, I grabbed Phoenix, and Alvin grabbed me. I teleported the four of us back to my room in the academy.

I passed out afterwards.

What? I did say I only had the strength for one last teleport. Oh well. The Academy saw that I was taken care of, and then, it came time for me to leave for good.

Chapter 21

While in recovery the day after the battle, Simon was working on his own theory regarding magic. If a magician suffers from a spell over and over, then they are more likely to be resistant to that specific spell and faster to recover. He came up with that theory given that unlike last time, he was feeling better during the recovery process. Rather than remain in his bed in the medical ward, he paced around the room, with help from his cane.

Simon the Stylish certainly had a ring to it (not that modern magicians follow the pronoun then adjective format anymore). However, if he wanted this theory to be studied by students, then more testing was required. Simon laughed at the idea. He had enough suffering through soul draining attacks for his lifetime. Let someone else become famous from that theory.

Simon was worried to see that he was the only one in the medical ward. Last he heard, Archmage was supposed to recover here as well. If the poison from the Fang of Arachne took him, then it would be too late for those final farewells. Simon needed advice now, especially with Virgil now possessing Morgan.

The doors to the chamber opened and Simon turned to smile at Phoenix and Alvin.

"Visitors!" Simon exclaimed and limped in their direction. "I've been waiting for you two. I wanted one last conversation before I leave."

"You're going so soon?" Alvin asked

"I am. I can get by well enough back home."

"After what you've been through, you certainly have the freedom to decide that," Phoenix said with a nod. "I'll miss you."

"We're still going to stay in touch," Simon assured his friends.

"I hate to say it, but It's a shame that Morgan isn't part of the group," Alvin sighed. "Never thought she was the daughter of the enemy."

"She was a forgotten child," Simon noted.

"Where did you get that line from?" Phoenix questioned.

"From Alvin. It was one of his cryptic sleep prophecies. He even predicted Archmage's death. And there's that final line I still need to figure out: the upcoming battle is only the start of the path the aged magician walks." Phoenix and Alvin looked at each other during Simon's explanation. He blinked. "What are you two hiding from me?"

"He's not going to believe us unless we show him," Alvin reached into his coat's pocket. "Hang on. I keep a mirror here. Foresight purposes."

"A mirror?" Simon raised an eyebrow at the pair.

"No one's told you, it seems," Phoenix paused and took a moment to think. "We have good news and bad news for you. Which do you want first?"

"The good news."

"The good news is that Archmage is alive," Phoenix revealed. "I haven't talked with him, but last I saw, he was in his office."

"That's great!" Simon exclaimed. "I need to see him!"

"First, you need to see the bad news for yourself," Alvin held the mirror out to him.

Simon gasped when he saw his own reflection in the mirror. His eyes were sunken with dark gray circles and his cheeks were slightly wrinkled. Hesitantly, he lifted his top hat from his head, and sure enough, his hair was graying. Although he still had some black hair left, it was going to take more than plucking the gray hairs out to fix his condition.

"H-how?" Simon muttered.

"Your life was drained, which physically took away some of your remaining years," Phoenix explained. "I didn't notice it at first due to the darkness, but now, it's quite obvious. Normally, a magician who suffers such an attack passes away, so you are the first exception. I am not sure what this means for you moving on."

"At the very least, I know that I'm not dying anytime soon," Simon slowly grinned. "This is only the start of the path I walk down."

"You're taking this a lot better than I thought you would," Alvin noted.

"Ah, yes, but you forget that I am an illusionist," Simon grinned and put his hat back on. "I can make an illusion over my features."

"Wouldn't that take some of your concentration?" Phoenix pointed out.

"It certainly would, which is why I will practice it when I am around my family. You two take care. See you again soon."

Simon and Phoenix gave each other a half-hug, followed by another one with Alvin. These two stuck by him throughout the danger and put their lives on the line for a better, undead-free tomorrow. Simon owed them much and hoped that they would stay by his side wherever his path takes him. For now, although it pained him on the inside, they parted ways here, with Simon walking towards Archmage's office.

Simon was definitely surprised to see Archmage sitting by himself in his office. Even with Phoenix revealing he was alive; it was a shock to see it for himself. He opened the door and stepped inside to take a seat. Archmage had his eyes closed and his head reclined slightly. Simon gulped, thinking that the headmaster was dead. Slowly, he pointed his cane forward to touch him in the chest.

"I am very much alive, Mr. Crowley," Archmage said before the cane touched his chest. "I am trying to take a nap."

"That's a relief," Simon pulled his cane back with a sigh of relief. "But how are you here? Weren't you poisoned?"

"I still am," Archmage revealed. "I can only delay the poison through sheer power. For how long, I know not, but it will kill me one day. Perhaps it will kill me tomorrow. But enough about morbidity. Congratulations on defeating Darius. Professor Brenton is escorting him to the Antarctic Academy for Magicians for punishment."

"About that bat-" Simon stopped himself. "Antarctic Academy for Magicians?"

"There is an academy on each continent."

"Isn't that still a pocket dimension?"

"It is, but it feels colder. Now, what were you saying?"

Simon breathed in through his nose, first trying to wrap his frustration around the logic of the Antarctic Academy. One problem at a time though.

"I think Virgil possessed Morgan," Simon explained. "I think he realized that having a rotting corpse for a body. Please, tell me it isn't possible that he did."

"She touched his phylactery, so it is," Archmage noted. "This is a big problem. I will have to talk with an old friend regarding this. He will certainly have something to say to know that Virgil is back among the living."

"Oh, and is that friend Santiago Salvador?" Simon joked and chuckled.

"He prefers to go by Salvie."

Simon stopped laughing. "That doesn't even phase me in the slightest. Not after everything I have seen and been through."

"I will start to consult the old tomes of necromancy to see if there's a way to undo a possession. Afterwards, we can destroy Virgil, and then see that Morgan is punished alongside her father."

"Is that last part really necessary?" Simon asked. "It was Virgil we fought, not Morgan."

"And it was Morgan who stabbed me, not Virgil," Archmage pointed out. "Regardless of what she has become, she did that out of her own free will."

Simon sighed. "I understand. But go easy on the punishment. No imprisonments in Antarctica.

"I'll think about it. Of course, if you were willing to take my power, you could decide whether or not Morgan should be punished. Is that a sacrifice you are willing to make?"

Simon thought it over. He knew that this was a topic Archmage would bring up again and that he should have been prepared for it. As much as he hated to reject someone who was dying, Simon was set on his choice. Archmage would have to live with it and find a new student to take his power.

Still, his story was only beginning.

"I defeated Darius without your power," Simon started. "It took a lot out of me, but I managed it on my own. I will not forget your kindness to my family, but unfortunately, I cannot take your power. Still, you can bet that I will involve myself with finishing what I started. Just as I found a way to defeat Darius on my own, I will find a way to save Morgan and destroy Virgil on my own."

"I wouldn't expect anything else from you," Archmage smirked. "Your method is one of the reasons I wanted you to replace me. Perhaps one day, you shall change your mind. Or maybe I will move on or die before giving power. It may be time for the legacy of the Archmage to end."

"Your legacy will never end," Simon assured him. "Not as long as this academy remains."

"Of course," Archmage finally opened his eyes, which looked at the student warmly. "I wish you would stay to finish your studies, but given your history, I knew it was only a matter of time before you dropped out."

"That there was definitely a burn." Simon laughed.

"It is what it is," Archmage extended his hand forward. "This certainly won't be the last we meet."

"I wouldn't hope for anything else."

Simon shook hands with Archmage firmly. Although they had their disagreements, he was thankful for Archmage's presence. Without him, Simon would have never learned about the world of magic. Real magic, that is. It was time to move on from his simple parlor tricks. He was ready to see what was next.

Archmage closed his eyes to return to his nap. Simon stood up from his chair and walked out of the office quietly. He was ready to teleport back home when he saw one last person he needed to say goodbye to. Cassandra walked towards him, no longer hiding behind the illusion of Professor Murdoch. Without her teachings, Simon would have never defeated Darius. He owed her as much as he did Archmage and Phoenix.

"Good to see you before you leave," Cassandra smiled. "I won't keep you from your family for too long. I just wanted to thank you for doing what I couldn't find the strength to."

"It's no prob-"

"Catch!"

Cassandra flicked a small object at him. Simon fumbled for it with one hand before he was able to catch it. In the palm of his hands was a small purple badge, much like students who have finished learning illusions had. Simon looked up to thank Cassandra only to see that she was missing. Of course, she had taught him everything he needed to know. It was time to move on.

Simon pinned the button to the brim of his hat and teleported back home.

.

After that day, I was one of two students to have dropped out of the North American Academy for Magicians. As much as I would have liked to be the first and set history, that honor goes to Morgan. Oh well. At least I get to have the honor of being the first to follow that trend.

That's another lesson to keep in mind: always find a way to take credit for something. Never lie and take credit for something you didn't do but you are allowed to stretch out the truth as much as you can. Taking credit leaves you with a sense of pride that helps deal with any of those emotional problems you're dealing with.

So, I will gladly take credit for being the first to follow the trend of dropping out of magic school. It certainly helped me deal with the emotions that came with knowing that once again, I was a dropout. Mom and Dad would be so proud.

At the very least, they were proud that I was back home. And I was here to stay.

I did share the story of what happened with my family. That includes all of my brothers and sisters. Now, don't get me wrong, I didn't tell them the whole truth. I greatly exaggerated much of the battles and never once mentioned the pain I went through (I was thankful to have illusions to cover my face). Most of them were too young to understand what has happened, but when they are older, I will tell them the truth.

Of course, I couldn't hide the truth from my parents, and Scott played a crucial part in the story already. They knew the whole deal. My parents were naturally worried for me, for both what I have been through and what I had planned next. Scott wasn't particularly worried. The experience did mend that broken bridge between us.

And I will admit that I wasn't sure what I was going to do with my future.

I spent time with my family during the holidays. I went back to the streets and fell back on a few old tricks. I even started to hang out with Zack and his gang, who were starting to veer away from crime.

Zack had the same problems about his future. We both had no clue where we were going with it. At one point, Zack joked about him and I going into business together. He thought that given our performance stopping the necromancers, we could be heroes.

That idea actually sounded very tempting. The Stylish Simon and Zack Attack has a very nice ring to it.

I wanted to put my talents to good use. Thankfully, an unexpected Christmas gift gave me the opportunity to start on that path.

Chapter 22

Just like many other households, the Crowley family always wakes up early in the morning on Christmas. Only Simon and Scott knew that there was no Santa and that their parents bought the gifts under the pine tree in the living room. Still, they knew better than to ruin the magic of the holidays for their younger siblings. They joined in on the act and woke up early in the morning with everyone else. Simon cast an illusion on himself to appear more youthful (as it was his habit now) and followed Seth to the living room with Scott.

No one was expecting the mass of presents that flowed out from underneath the tree. Their parents bought two or three presents per child, but now, there was more than that. Simon could not help but smile when Seth jumped into the pile along with his sisters and brother. The parents were cautious at first, but when they saw that there was nothing nefarious about the gifts, they let their children have fun.

"He actually came through," Simon thought out loud.

"But how?" Scott whispered.

"Magic," Simon held back a laugh.

"Of course you say that," Scott rolled his eyes but smiled.

In all honesty, Simon liked thinking that Archmage dressed up as Santa and snuck into the house with a sack of presents. It was unlikely, but at the very least, it gave him some joy. Scott joined the others in the present pile, and with a sigh of relief, Simon joined them. From toys to art supplies to video games, there was something for everyone.

Yet, the only thing that Simon had was a sealed envelope.

"Strange," his father noted. "Maybe your presents are under the wrapping?"

"I have a feeling that I am going to find out otherwise."

Simon tore the envelope open. Inside was a single bronze key and a piece of parchment. There was no writing on the parchment, only an elaborate circle with different runes. Scott walked over to his brother and peeked over his shoulder to see what the deal was.

"Is that some strange magician's code?" Scott asked.

"No, it's a circle," Simon answered. "Surprisingly enough, magicians don't have a secret language."

"That's lame."

"Very lame, but honestly, not the lamest thing I have learned over the past few months," Simon glanced at the circle again. "Scottie, get dressed. We're going on a little field trip."

It took the two boys a couple of minutes to get dressed up in long sleeved t-shirts and jeans. Simon thought that he was going to miss his old school uniform, but as time went by, he realized that trench coats were overdoing it for a magician who fought physically rather than with magic. He did need to find a new style to reflect who he was but that was a subject for another time.

After they got dressed, Simon grabbed Scott by the shoulder. Scott looked oddly at his brother, who focused on the circle on the parchment. He concentrated, and after a few seconds, the two were whisked away from their home to a new situation. How clever of an idea it was to draw a teleportation circle.

At first, the two brothers were surrounded in darkness. Yet, when they carefully stepped out of the circle, the lights came on. The two were in a small bedroom with a twin bed, wardrobe, and chest. Off to the side of the room was a desk with a journal, and to the back was a door slightly ajar to lead to the bathroom. Simon's Christmas presents were on the bed.

"Woah," Scott looked around in awe. "This is incredible."

"Scott, we're in a bedroom. What's incredible about that?"

"We teleported here. You have your own room that you can access with magic."

"I had my own room which I could access by magic back at the academy. I just don't have a roommate this time. Hang on. I'm going to look around."

Simon walked over to the second door in the room and opened it. They were in an apartment. Aside from the bedroom, there was no other furniture. Just a lot of empty space. Sunlight peered in through the open windows to show the emptiness. Simon stepped into the room, and suddenly, Archmage was in the center of the room, looking back at him.

"Archmage?" Simon gasped.

"Mr. Crowley," Archmage greeted. "Merry Christmas, by the way, I wanted to see you one last time and explain the gift I have for you."

"Thanks for the new gaming system, by the way," Scott quickly said.

"You're quite welcome, Mr. Scott Crowley," Archmage smiled.

"And as much as I hate to be selfish, but what about my gift?" Simon asked.

"Allow me to explain. After our last conversation, I had a lot to think about. Specifically, on whether we should help each other regarding how to handle the scheming of Virgil the Damned. Although I appreciate your methods, we may have disagreements on the end results. Therefore, I have settled on a compromise. I will not directly aid you but I will not stop you either."

"So, you're going to do nothing then?" Simon asked.

"Not quite. You need space for your search. Something private and away from your family. I have provided you with an apartment for such a space and have moved your gifts and any other belongings here. It is two blocks away from where your family lives. That is my gift to you."

"He really goes out for Christmas," Scott commented.

"Of course, once you turn eighteen, you will have to find a way to pay rent."

"And there's the catch!" Simon smiled.

"Still, at the very least, you can begin your search for Virgil the Damned in peace. You can decorate the place however you like. You may also show your true self here and not worry about projecting that illusion."

"True self?" Scott turned to Simon, who dropped his illusions. "What happened to you?!"

"Life drain attack. Very painful," Simon replied.

"Asides from Virgil, you may hear of other threats. You may want to find a way to confront these threats. Virgil isn't the only villain around. I just felt compelled to warn you."

"Thanks a lot," Simon frowned.

"It's no problem at all, Mr. Crowley. Asides from the accommodations in the bedroom, I have left one final gift. Something I feel you will enjoy. Take care."

Archmage smiled at Simon one last time, then disappeared without any trace. Simon wasn't sure what to think. He was grateful for the living space, and with it, he had ideas on how to be able to pay for furniture and for rent once he was an adult. Yet, Archmage was expecting that he would fight in the battles. The war that the magicians fought in, he realized. He was hesitant to fight someone's else's battle.

But it was his battle. It had been his battle ever since he started to train as a magician. He had a duty.

"You know, I think I would like to be a student of Archmage," Scott noted with a smile. "Can you put in a good word for me?"

"Perhaps," Simon continued to think. "Scottie, can you get Zack for me?"

"Uh, sure," Scott walked towards the front door. "Why?"

"I think going into business together may be possible soon," Simon told him. "Be sure to mention that. I'll talk to you soon."

When Scott left the apartment, Simon walked back into his bedroom. He approached his new desk to see a journal and a pen on it. He flipped through the journal to see entirely blank pages. Simon smirked. This was his journal, and just as the magicians of the past had done, it was his duty to record his life in it. Perhaps a future generation of students would study from it, much like Edwin the Expressive or Watson the Wanderer.

Simon clicked the pen open and dubbed the journal with its title.

The Adventures of THE STYLISH SIMON!

Well, there you have it. That's the story of how I discovered magic, studied how to use it, and ultimately, how I fought with it.

Of course, this is not only the start of my story, but that of many of my friends as well; both the people you see here and the others I have yet to write about. But I am sure that if you loved this, and if I am ever given another chance to write it, you will enjoy my other adventures.

Now, to all the disbelievers who made it this far, magic is real. And if you still don't believe me, come to Santiago's Shield and I will show you that it is real. I'll be right, you'll be wrong, and we'll go our separate ways.

To all of the believers (and the disbelievers turned believers) of magic, I hope you take more out of this other than that magic is real. I opened up to you both my triumphs and my defeats. I have also left behind the different life lessons I have learned, both before and after taking up magic. If you have struggled with these problems before, please apply my lessons.

And finally, a message to all of the magicians who seek to abuse magic. First off, I greatly appreciate how you read my story all the way to the end. Hey, I won't judge my fans. However, I am going to ask that you stop with the misuse of magic.

Alright, even I admit that contradicts what I just said.

But I mean it. Stop with your evil ways. I say this as a warning, for if your plans ever come into conflict with my friends or family, it's game over for you.

Right. No reason to leave on such a dire warning. So, on a lighter note, if you do manage to find me, I will sign your copy of the book.

What? Were you expecting a recommendation letter for the North American Academy for Magicians? Or were you expecting me to take you on as a student? Well, let's just say both of those are stories for another time.

Respectfully,

Simon Crowley (AKA THE STYLISH SIMON!)

ACKNOWLEDGMENTS

What a crazy six years and who knows how many failed book projects it has been to get here. This wouldn't have been possible without my parents, Kevin and Charlsie Prosser. They have been my biggest supporters since the start, and I have never once heard them talk me out of writing. Even when I jumped from idea to idea and never finished what I started; I wouldn't be who I am without them.

Among my teachers, there have been two who had the biggest impact on my life: Dawn Prosser and Scott Collins. Aunt Dawn, who was my middle school math teacher for two years, helped me with the transition from homeschool to public school, and didn't mind when I kept calling her Ms. Prosser for a year after she stopped teaching. Mr. Collins, my high school newspaper teacher for two years, set me on my path to journalism while teaching me the importance of deadlines and the shortness of AP style, of which I partially mimic with my narratives today.

While he may not have realized this while teaching the one class I had him for, Professor Robert Howard gave me the idea for a new way to write. All Professor Howard did was define what an epistolary novel was, and that set me on a new direction with my writing.

Although we have never met in person, I would like to note that Charles Stacy did play a big role in helping me. As

I was writing, he watched, and was quick to point out the mistakes I've made. Whenever I made a mistake, he would always point it out, and served as a confidant with whom I could share my ideas with.

Additionally, I would like to thank the unnamed roleplaying group that Charles and I are a part of online. Once more, these are people who I have never met. Yet they are among the first who witnessed Simon Crowley as a character, and he was quick to become a fan favorite.

While I may be a writer, I am not an artist. Thankfully, Rebekah Nelson was able to design the wonderful cover for the book. Without her, I wouldn't even know where to begin to look for a cover. I hope that our partnership can continue when it comes to any future projects that need covers.

A huge concern I had after the editing phase was figuring out how to publish a book. I tried searching up online and found that it was rather difficult. I would like to thank Amazon, for providing a way for authors to publish their books that is easy. I would also like to thank Monti Washington, who, during our brief meeting, encouraged me to self-publish with Amazon by sharing his experiences with it.

One of my biggest obstacles with writing is writer's block. Thankfully, to get through it, I jam out to music. There are too many musicians to thank, and I am pretty confident that even if I list them, none of them will see it. But for the record, two of the big names were Ed Sheeran and Lin-Manuel Miranda.

I would like to point out that before writing this, I knew absolutely nothing about magic. So, a big shout-out to all of the people who regularly post how-tos on WikiHow, blogs, or other websites. They were able to help me bring the magic to my narrative.

Among my inspirations, I would like to acknowledge Ernest Hemingway and Stan Lee. Before learning more about Hemingway, my narrative was long, dull, and boring. From reading him, I started to write shorter paragraphs and conversations that pushed the story along. Stan Lee was a hero to me that passed away while I wrote. It has always been my dream to write about superheroes such as those Lee created, and I hope that this is a good start.

I would like to thank Chris Baty, the founder of National Novel Writing Month (NaNoWriMo). This book was my entry for 2018, and the second to be completed on time. NaNoWriMo brings out a competitive side of me to race against time, which sees that I complete my projects.

I am thankful for the opportunities I have had and give my thanks to God. My blessings come from him and I will continue my effort to do good.

Finally, there is my grandfather, Robert Prosser. I never visited as much as I would have liked, but I still miss him today. There are many things I could talk about, but the one that sticks out the most would be the small talks we've had. It showed that he did care about me, and so, I have chosen to dedicate this book in his memory.

ABOUT THE AUTHOR

Chance Prosser has always dreamed about being a writer and has worked on various projects over several years. The House of Virgil is one project he started from start to finish as part of National Novel Writing Month. He was inspired to write this story from a tabletop roleplaying game revolving around teen superheroes and hopes to expand on a new series with future projects. Chance is currently a student at Baker University, studying Mass Media to pursue a career in radio while being able to write books and record podcasts in his free time. He also maintains his own website, Chancethepodcaster.com, to post updates on his writing, podcast, and videos.

Made in the USA
Monee, IL
14 July 2020